Norstead was not in a joking mood as he said, "In my opinion, the situation is on the brink of being calamitous. This latest piece of intelligence that the Soviets have a cell operating in Jerusalem —and a *Mokryye Dela* unit at that— complicates the entire situation." He gave Camellion a long admiring look. "I'm still wondering how you managed to escape from those two Russians who tried to put the snatch on you! They were the best— or don't you know what *Mokryye Dela* means in Russian?"

Camellion shrugged and glanced at his watch. "I had no choice," he said simply. "I wasn't in the mood to die. *Mokryye Dela?* I believe the phrase refers to the GRU's 'Department of Wet Affairs'."

"The phrase means just that," Ethan Friedenthal confirmed solemnly. "Literally translated, '*Mokryye Dela*' means 'wet,' and in this case it means 'blood wet'—terror and assassination!"

"Which means that we can be positive of one thing," Langbein added. "The Russian agents in the Holy City are there, probably, for purposes of mass murder!"

"And the sooner we hit them, the better!" Camellion concluded.

DEATH MERCHANT:
THE PSYCHOTRON PLOT

by
Joseph Rosenberger

PINNACLE BOOKS • NEW YORK CITY

Dedicated to a people whose rock-hard faith
has outlived the long slow passage of centuries . . .

CHAPTER I

All during the flight from Paris to Tel-Aviv, the beefy, square-jawed man who sat next to Monsieur Paul Lavone and introduced himself as Matt Gallanger from Houston, Texas, had been a first class bore, never for a moment ceasing in his garrulous efforts to draw the Frenchman into conversation. A boisterous, outgoing man, who seemingly was oblivious to Lavone's reluctance to engage in a tete-a-tete, the gabby Gallanger insisted on boasting about his knowledge of Israel.

"Yes sir," he said expansively, puffing on a big cigar, "I went out and got me a book on Israel before coming over here. Figured I'd study up on the country I was going to take a vacation in. Sure am going to enjoy it too. First vacation I've had in seven years. Thought I'd come over here and see what them Zionists and A-rabs is fighting over."

Without turning his head from the window, where he was watching an ocean of cumuli clouds churn far below, Lavone said drily, his voice tinged with a thick accent, "Monsieur, you mean Israelis, not Zionists."

Gallanger glanced in annoyance at the Frenchman, who was dressed in a powder-blue suit. "So what the hell's the difference. They're all Jews, ain't they?"

With a trace of a smile, Lavone turned to the Texan, wondering what the man would think if he knew he was actually talking to Richard Joseph Camellion, the world famous Death Merchant, but he said, "The difference is that the Zionists hold officially that Israel is the home of all Jews everywhere, as is made clear by the Law of Return and the Law of Citizenship. But an Israeli who is not a Zionist usually says, 'I'm an Israeli first and a Jew second,' all of which creates a lot of confusion."

The heavy-set Texan chuckled. "Well now, I sure didn't know that," he said, nodding his head slowly. " 'Course, I know that Tel-Aviv is really two cities—right, old buddy? Tel-Aviv and—what's the other one? Yeah. Jaffa. Right?"

Still affecting his role as a French businessman, Camellion nodded.

5

"But how come?" Gallanger demanded. "How come Tel-Aviv is really two cities?"

"Jaffa dates back to possibly 2,000 years before Christ," Camellion explained in a bored manner, "while Tel-Aviv is comparatively new, having been founded in 1909 by Zionist settlers. Now if you don't mind, Monsieur Gallanger, I'd appreciate a termination to our conversation. We'll land in an hour or so, and I'd like to take a nap. I'm very tired."

An expression of surprise crossed Gallanger's friendly-looking face. "Sure thing, pardner," he said jovially. "You just lean right back there and catch yourself forty winks." He leaned closer, nudged Camellion in the ribs and, with a snicker, whispered, "You can dream of them sexy steward-esses; them little gals sure know how to shake it up for a man."

Gallanger turned quickly to a stewardess who was passing down the aisle. "Say there, Miss," he called out. "Bring me another double bourbon and water. Yes, sir, this here airline has sure got mighty good whiskey."

In disgust, Camellion leaned back and closed his eyes, sleep coming quickly. He dozed fitfully, and didn't fully awaken until the El-Al Israel Airlines 747 jet was circling for a landing at Lod International Airport in Tel-Aviv, when Gallanger began shaking him. "Time to fasten your seat belt, pardner," the man grinned. "We're coming down. I sure hope this big critter makes it! This is sure a lot of airplane!"

"Merci, Monsieur," Camellion mumbled as he fastened his seat belt. Then the long runway, on which flickered phantasmal heat devils, began rushing up like a giant flat blanket of gray. A slight jar as the landing gear touched the runway, as rubber tires made contact with hot July concrete . . . a whirring of the tremendous engines as the pilot eased back on the throttle and cut the fuel. Finally the El-Al 747 came to a complete stop. The Death Merchant relaxed. His mission had begun.

Unbuckling his seat belt, Gallanger said, "By golly, we made it! Say pardner, I've got hotel reservations at the Dan." He laughed rather nervously. "Don't know the location of the Dan Hotel, but I suppose the cab drivers will. Yes, sir . . . I'd sure hate to get lost in this man's town. I was thinking that if you was going my way we could share the same cab . . ."

Gallanger stood up, all the while giving Camellion little sideway glances.

Picking up his attache case, the Death Merchant did some rapid thinking. He also had reservations at the Dan, and although he didn't relish the prospect of riding into Tel-Aviv with the ill-mannered Gallanger—why not? The man's presence, at least for the comparatively short distance to the hotel, would lend greater credibility to the Death Merchant's cover. Even Russian intelligence agents would never expect him to be in the company of such an obvious clod. Why Gallanger even wore a broad-brimmed Stetson! But no Western-styled boots, though his suit had that Western touch. What a joker!

Camellion made up his mind: It would be a simple matter for him to disengage himself from the man after they reached the Dan, before going to the Shin-Bet "contact" house on Shivte Yisrael street in Jaffa.

Smiling, Camellion said pleasantly, "Oui, Monsieur. I should be delighted to share a Sherut with you into Tel-Aviv. I, too, am staying at the Dan Hotel."

Gallanger's thin brows narrowed. "Share—a what?"

"A Sherut," Camellion said patiently. "An Israeli service taxi." He moved out into the aisle and began following Gallanger from the aircraft, his ever-moving eyes scanning faces and surroundings . . . alert for danger, probing for anything unusual. Without his twin .357 Magnums he felt naked, as though his very soul were exposed. Certainly, without his weapons, he was very vulnerable, and would be until he reached the contact house. However, the choice had not been his to make. To have carried the Magnum revolvers on the El-Al jet would have been asking for all sorts of trouble. Should anyone have seen them—the officials of the airline would have had no way of knowing that he was working for the Shin-Bet, the Intelligence Service of their nation. No . . . it would have been too dangerous to carry the Magnums on the plane.

Passing through Israeli Customs, picking up their luggage and having their dollars changed into Israeli pounds (I£4.20 to the dollar) at the Tel-Aviv Bank's airport branch were simple matters; and soon "Paul Lavone" and his rubbernecking American friend were in the taxi area, standing impatiently on the curb in the hot sun. Almost immediately a service taxi—a 1969 Plymouth—pulled up, and, after the driver placed their luggage in the trunk, Gallanger stepped

7

to one side, permitting the Death Merchant to enter the cab first.

Other than the driver—a dark-skinned man with a small pointed beard—another man was in the service car, a middle-thirties, moon-faced individual with jet-black hair and heavily-lidded eyes. Sitting in the back seat, the man glared up at Camellion, and suddenly the Death Merchant knew! Even as he was sitting down, he realized, knowing instantly with an intuitive sense nurtured by years of living within the bitter breath of death, that like a damn fool he had walked directly into a clever trap that had been extremely well planned—simple but amazingly effective; and before he had time to relax, the sharp-featured creep was pressing a pistol firmly against his side, a 9 MM Radom Parabellum with a long Russian-type silencer. In spite of the clinging heat, the Death Merchant felt an icy wave race through his lean, hard body—*TRAPPED!*

"Don't move a single muscle, Camellion!" the man with the Radom said in a low voice. "We want to take you alive, but we'll kill you if we can't."

Not commenting, Camellion settled back, thinking of John Cecil Evers, the CIA agent who had been his contact in Paris. Only Evers had known the disguise the Death Merchant would be using and the flight he'd be taking from Paris to Tel-Aviv. The thought was a sickening one, but there was no escaping the final conclusion: Evers had to be a double-agent, which meant also that GRU, the Soviet Union's worldwide intelligence and espionage apparatus—the military counter-part of the infamous KGB—had infiltrated the Central Intelligence Agency. Camellion felt almost nauseated. How many more Soviet agents were scattered throughout the ranks of the CIA, or, for that matter, the Shin-Bet, the super-efficient Intelligence Service of the Israelis?

Mentally the Death Merchant congratulated the Russian whose portrayal of a Texan had been perfect; even the distinctive Texas drawl had been without a single flaw. Only now, as "Gallanger" spoke to the other GRU agent in the back seat, his voice was cultured and well modulated, without the least trace of Texas, USA . . .

"We don't have to worry about his attache case, Mikhail," the man who called himself Gallanger said. "I saw the contents when we passed through Customs—nothing but toilet articles, vitamins and a thermos of tomato juice."

Mikhail snickered. "Vitamins and tomato juice!" he said, giving a sadistic little laugh. "You won't be needing them where you're going, Death Merchant . . . only a lot of luck. Time has run out for you."

"Should I drive in to Tel-Aviv, or do you want me to go directly to Point B?" the driver asked, glancing quickly around at Gallanger, who, having reached behind the seat, pulled forth a .43 caliber Russian Zortov automatic pistol. Clicking off the safety, he shoved the muzzle against Camellion's other side.

"Point B," he said. "Turn the car around and drive toward Jerusalem, Anwar. When we get outside the city, I'll tell you where to go."

Gallanger pressed his gun hard against the Death Merchant's side. "By tomorrow you'll be on your way to Cairo, and that, my friend, will be the end of you."

Which means I'll be at the tender mercies of Colonel Kagorin, the Resident Agent of the Cairo Residentura Camellion thought bitterly, *but I think I'll change their plans for them . . .*

Anwar, the driver, whom Camellion knew to be an Arab, had turned the car around, now they were headed in the opposite direction from Tel-Aviv, southeast toward Jerusalem. Keeping his eyes in front of him and noticing that the traffic was getting thinner, Camellion said mildly, "I take it you gentleman belong to the Soviet State Security Service, or, more specifically, to *Glavnoye Razvedyvatelnoye*. I am further assuming that you're all 'legals' stationed in Cairo, with official cover and diplomatic immunity—with the exception of our Arab friend?"

Camellion noticed a flicker of admiration in Mikhail's cruel eyes at his use of the correct Russian title for GRU, but not for a fraction of a second did the Radom Parabellum waver, nor did Gallanger's pistol move from the Death Merchant's side, the muzzle pressing almost painfully just above the belt line.

Gallanger smiled thinly, and once more lapsed into a Texas drawl. "You're absolutely right, Camellion," he said pleasantly, nodding his head slightly. "Captain Boris Sokolovskii at your service—and on your other side, let me introduce Mikhail Tuvalov. But say, pardner, don't you think I did a rather good job at playing the part of an American Texan? It took me weeks to perfect this accent."

9

"Your Texas accent was very good," Camellion said honestly, "so good that it even fooled me. 'The Center' in Moscow should be proud of you."

"Thank you," Sokolovskii said, grinning. "Your own French accent wasn't bad." Then, abruptly, he laughed uproariously. "But imagine—YOU, of all people, pretending to be the representative of a toy manufacturer! That was good, Camellion, but . . . not quite good enough. You didn't fool us."

Camellion said, "I got the idea while I was in Moscow last year!" He sensed the two Russian GRU agents stiffen in surprise and resentment, and to further irk their professional pride, he used the Russian pronunciation for KGB, the Soviet Union's State Security Police. "Directly across from *Kah Gay Beh* headquarters at 2 Dezerzhinsky Street is *Detsky Mir*, or as we say in English, the 'Children's World,' a toy and department store."

Mikhail, the sullen GRU agent, spoke up, his voice tinged with indignation. "You were in Moscow last year, and that close to *Kah Gay Beh* headquarters! You swine! I don't believe it!"

Now it was the Death Merchant's turn to laugh. "Come now, Mikhail, you shouldn't feel insulted because I managed to slip in and out of your precious capitol. After all, we're all professionals here. We win some . . . we lose some . . ."

Sokolovskii said smugly, "And this time you've lost for good, Camellion. The final round is ours." The chunky Russian suddenly became very serious. "I'll give you some good advice, If I were in your precarious position, I'd cooperate with Colonel Kagorin, our Station Chief in Cairo. Why not be practical and die with as little pain as possible? Tell Kagorin all he wants to know and your death will be painless—a quick bullet in the back of the head. But believe me, you will tell us all you know about your mission for the CIA and the Shin-Bet . . . Kagorin will see to that . . . and he's an expert. He loves to hear strong men scream."

Pretending fear, Camellion let his voice quiver slightly. "You may be right, Sokolovskii. Kagorin's noted for his sadism."

He glanced out the window and saw that they were passing through a small village, and he knew that if he were to live, he'd have to make his move soon. Better to try and fail, to die now than be carted off to Cairo.

Camellion turned to Sokolovskii. "I don't suppose there's

10

any harm in asking for a cigarette." As he had anticipated, the man was instantly suspicious.

"You weren't smoking on the plane," he said coldly. "Why now?"

"I only smoke when I'm extremely nervous," Camellion lied, sighing deeply. "And right now I'm not exactly calm, as you should certainly understand."

Mikhail Tuvalov's mouth twisted into a malicious sneer. "It would seem the fearless Death Merchant is afraid to die, Boris," he joked. "He's like all *Amerikanskis:* all talk but no guts."

Camellion turned to him and said, "Not afraid to die, my Russian comrade. But dying now . . . it comes at such an inconvenient moment. I did want to see the sights of Tel-Aviv —and I've heard so much about how the Israelis prepare lamb. But I suppose I'll never get to taste *shashlik* or *machshi* . . . How about that cigarette?"

Once more Boris Sokolovskii laughed, obviously enjoying the Death Merchant's ironic sense of humor. "I have only cigars," he said good naturedly. "Mikhail, give him a cigarette. As he pointed out, we're all professionals. There's no reason why we should bear him any ill will or not show him the simple courtesies of life."

"Very well," Mikhail said reluctantly, giving Camellion a contemptuous look, "but keep zeroed in on him. I don't trust him."

Slowly, never taking his weasel eyes off Camellion, he shoved his Radom automatic into a shoulder holster, after which—just as carefully—he reached into his suit coat and pulled out a pack of cigarettes which he held out to Camellion. He watched the Death Merchant extract a cigarette, then lit it for him and dropped the lighter and the pack back into his pocket.

That's when Richard Camellion spit directly into the grinning face of Death and made his desperate bid for life, moving with such incredible speed that the two Russian agents were completely taken off guard.

After taking a few puffs to make sure the end was glowing, Camellion removed the cigarette from his mouth, and then, striking like a cobra, just as Mikhail was reaching for his weapon once more, he jabbed the burning end of the cigarette into the astonished Russian's face, aiming for the center of

11

the man's right eyeball. He missed—damn it!—the burning end sizzling against the corner of Mikhail's eye.

The Death Merchant's attack was two-pronged, for even as Mikhail screamed in agony, Camellion, with all the strength that he could muster, rammed his right elbow against Boris Sokolovskii's gun-hand, pinning the Russian's wrist and the gun to the back of the seat. With almost the same split-second motion, Camellion moved his body slightly forward and stabbed Sokolovskii in the eyes with two forked fingers of his left hand, jumping slightly as Sokolovskii's finger squeezed the trigger of his automatic from sheer reflex. With a muffled boom the Zortov pistol went off, but since the muzzle was pressed into the back of the seat, the bullet buried itself harmlessly in the leather cushions.

Although Boris Sokolovskii was as strong as an angered bull, the searing pain in his eyes and his temporary tear-induced blindness put him at a terrible disadvantage as he struggled for the pistol and, at the same time, clawed at his eyes.

"KI-LL HIM, MIKHAIL!" he choked. "KILL THE SON OF A BITCH!"

With his mouth twisting and air whistling oddly through his nostrils, Mikhail pressed a palm to his burned eye and, gasping in pain, reached for his weapon with his other hand. The Death Merchant, however, was fully prepared for such a desperate move. He knew he had very little time, only a matter of seconds, and he hoped the blow would be effective . . .

For almost three years the Death Merchant had diligently practiced a left-handed judo chop, a blow that, in order to be effective, was almost impossible for a right-handed individual.

Savagely, as he stiffened his fingers, Camellion brought his left arm back until the inside bend of the elbow was almost touching his chin, and then he let the Russian have it, chopping him with all his strength across the upper lip.

There was a popping sound—like twigs snapping—as the side of the Death Merchant's hand connected with Mikhail's lip . . . as startled teeth broke away from the upper jawbone. "Ullllllllll!" the Russian gurgled in pain.

At the same time, Boris managed to free his gun-hand from Camellion's elbow, bringing up the weapon and trying to turn the muzzle toward Camellion, who grabbed the .43

Zortov with his other hand and pushed it up toward the roof of the car, away from his body.

On the other side of the Death Merchant, Mikhail's one hand dropped from his Radom, the other from his eye, the corner of which harbored an ugly red burn, and he grabbed his mouth spurting blood and knocked-out teeth. Pain replaced caution and, holding his hands tightly over his shattered mouth, he bent forward slightly, rocking back and forth in agony and making gurgling sounds.

Again the Death Merchant's hand slashed out, an arcing blur that suddenly materialized into the edge of a steel-hard hand that connected behind Mikhail's right ear. A long "Ahhhhhhh" whooshed out of the Russian and he collapsed, falling over like a toppled tree against Camellion, who now was battling Boris Sokolovskii for possession of the .43 Zortov.

Anwar had been glancing fearfully toward the back seat. Now he turned his head again, still uncertain as to the course of action he should pursue. Should he pull over to the side of the road and give his Russian employers a hand? That would have been the logical thing to do. But Anwar knew he couldn't, because on either side of the highway, tending crops, were scores of Kibbutzniks from the nearby *Ma'ale Hahamisha Kibbutz*. Surely they would come over to the car if he stopped, especially when they saw the struggle.

Anwar realized something else: Should the Israelis from the Kibbutz discover that he, a Syrian, was working with Russian intelligence agents— *By Allah!* They would certainly execute him as a spy!

The drive for self-preservation told Anwar what he must do—*drive on!* Continue along the road until they were out of sight of the Kibbutz. Let the Russians battle the crazy American, Anwar told himself. Somehow I'll save my own skin . . .

Boris Sokolovskii had been successful in bringing his gun arm down and was attempting to twist the deadly black muzzle toward Camellion's stomach. Furiously the two men struggled for the weapon, for Life itself, their faces—showing the result of their straining—only a foot apart, their eyes locked in hellish hatred, their jaw muscles contorting in determination. Finally, ever so slowly, the muzzle of the pistol began turning in Camellion's direction, while Sokolovskii, grinning like a devil incarnate, snarled in a labored

13

whisper, "I—I'm going to—to kill you . . . you American bastard . . ."

The Death Merchant was only seconds from Infinity—and knew it! He also knew that if he were to live, he would have to have an instant advantage. He found one when Sokolovskii, in order to better apply more strength, moved his body, pushing out one leg to brace himself against the back of the front seat. With all his strength, the Death Merchant stomped on the Russian's left instep. Instinctively, Boris' attention was diverted, and for a split second the pain in his foot made the muscles in his arm relax. But that tiny blink of eternity was all Camellion needed. Drawing on his rapidly dwindling reservoir of strength, he twisted the pistol back toward Sokolovskii until finally the muzzle was pressing into the man's guts, several inches below his belt buckle. Gradually, Camellion's hand tightened over Sokolovskii's fingers, squeezing them around the butt of the weapon. The Russian could not withstand the pressure. His trigger finger contracted, and the .43 Zortov went off.

The shot was not as muffled as the previous one that had sent a slug into the back of the seat, but sound had nothing to do with the direction of the present hunk of steel, which plowed upward through the Russian's stomach into his heart. Boris Sokolovskii looked very surprised. His mouth worked crazily, and for a moment it seemed he might even smile. But he didn't. Instead, his face relaxed, his eyes closed, and he died. He even looked peaceful as he slumped against the side of the car . . . except for the heavy stream of scarlet that had begun pouring from one corner of his mouth.

Glancing in the rear-view mirror, Anwar saw what had happened. Instantly, panic replaced common sense and, stupidly, he tried to jerk out his own pistol. The Death Merchant was too fast for him. He jerked the Radom from the unconscious Mikhail's shoulder holster and pressed it heavily against the back of Anwar's grimy neck.

"You know better than that, dumb-bell," Camellion said quietly. "Hand me your gun, but use only your thumb and forefinger when you take it out. Then you can turn this car around and drive me to Jaffa! I can't very well march you and my friend back here into the Dan at gunpoint."

Trembling, Anwar passed his weapon back to Camellion —a Beretta 9 MM. Then, shaking to such an extent that he could hardly drive, he turned the Plymouth around and

14

headed back in the direction of Tel-Aviv. Finally, he mustered the courage to ask, "What are you going to do with me?" Then very quickly—"I'll talk! I'll tell you anything you want to know . . ."

"Your fate will be decided by the Israelis," Camellion replied. "Cooperate with them and you might live. Try anything with me, and you'll not see today's sunset."

Richard Camellion leaned back in the seat. Glancing at the dead Sokolovskii, he pulled the pistol from the corpse's stiffening fingers and stuck it in his belt. It was then he noticed that M'khail, the other Russian agent in the back seat, was beginning to stir, groaning in a low voice. Camellion clipped him over the head with the barrel of the Beretta, and once more M'khail slumped.

Camellion relaxed, keeping the Beretta in his hand and his eyes on Anwar, whom he knew to be a coward—cowards were always upredictable. He thought of the mission that had brought him to Israel, remembering vividly the briefing he had had with the Director of the Central Intelligence Agency. Jacob Hemms had surprised the Death Merchant by asking him what he knew about extrasensory perception.

Intrigued, Camellion had stared curiously at the scholarly-looking CIA chief. Always blunt and to the point, Hemms was not a man to waste time with idle conversation. He stared back at Camellion, waiting for him to speak.

"ESP?" Camellion said, "or parapsychology, or what some call Psi. Or, to be technical, an awareness of, or response to, an external event or influences not apprehended by sensory means." He smiled broadly. "Don't tell me that's why you sent for me—to have me help the CIA in paranormal research?"

Hemms puffed thoughtfully on his pipe, then carefully placed it in an ashtray on his massive desk. "Even if we were starting an ESP lab, I think we'd have a difficult time catching up with the Russians," he said very seriously. "For years, the Soviet Union has been supporting research into parapsychology—and on no small basis either. As we understand it, their budget for ESP in 1971 was almost 28-million rubles."

"The Russians have always been practical in such matters," Camellion offered.

"Especially so in their ESP research," Hemms continued grimly. "They're directing their efforts toward the use of ESP, their aim being its technological application. And what

15

are we doing? Here in the United States, ESP research as a whole has only recently emerged from the basis of establishing statistical proof for ESP's existence, all of which should give you some idea of how far behind we are."

The Death Merchant's gaze locked with Hemms' brown eyes. "Are you telling me that the Ruskies have come up with some sort of weapons system involving ESP?"

Nodding slowly, Hemms picked up his pipe and said, "Psychical research in the Soviet Union is regarded as a new field in the natural sciences and is linked with bionics, biology, physics, etc. The Soviets refer to ESP as 'bioinformation,' 'biotelecommunication,' 'biocybernetics,' and what have you; and another thing, top Soviet scientists in biochemistry, neurology, electrical engineering, and many other hard sciences are recruited to explore the various aspects of Psi-riddles. In short, Richard, I'm telling you that parapsychology in the Soviet Union is highly respected, and—unlike in the U.S.—assigned top talent and major financial backing."

"All right, you've told me," Camellion said impatiently. "Now suppose you stop the lecture and tell me what you want."

Hemms smiled laconically. "I believe when I tell you what the Russians have done, you'll realize why it took their top brains to develop this weapon, which the Shin-Bet euphemistically calls 'The Mind Blaster!' Technically, the weapon is called the Psychotron. Anyhow, that's how the Russians refer to it, from what we've been able to learn."

Inhaling sharply, the Death Merchant sat up straight on the leather chair. Well now, the Shin-Bet! So the Israeli Intelligence Service was in on the act!

"Tell me about this Mind Blaster," Camellion said. He locked his hands behind his head, stretched out his legs and leaned back in the deep chair, gazing abstractedly at a sign on the opposite wall, over Hemms' desk:

Yes, though I walk through the valley of the Shadow of Death, I shall fear no evil, because I'm the meanest SOB in the valley.

Hemms chuckled and adjusted his glasses, pushing them up on his nose. "I rather assumed my mentioning the Shin-Bet would rekindle slumbering fires in you. You always did enjoy working with the best."

Folding his hands on the desk, Hemms became very serious. "According to the Shin-Bet, the Russians have a

16

secret base in Egypt, somewhere in the vicinity of Suez, and that's where they're experimenting with The Mind Blaster, a weapon that, by interfering with the electro-magnetic field of the human body, particularly of the brain, can cause delusions, hallucinations, and even death. Already in testing the hellish weapon, the Russians have driven insane the hundred or so inhabitants of Bel Sida, a tiny village in the Sinai Desert. Fortunately, at present, the Mind Blaster is only effective at short range, perhaps twenty or thirty miles —at maximum."

Analytically, Hemms searched the Death Merchant's expressionless face, in an attempt to probe the depths of those icy blue eyes. As usual, Hemms detected only a glint of frigid intelligence . . . and a strangeness that made him shift uncomfortably in his swivel chair; but he felt that unique apprehensiveness every time he looked directly into the diamond-hard eyes of the Death Merchant. Damn it! It was as if he were staring into a mirror of infinity.

Hemms cleared his throat and said, "But I have more bad news for you, Richard. When perfected, *the Mind Blaster will be capable of telepathic hypnosis!* Do I have to tell you what that means? Should the Russians ever be able to hypnotize thousands of people—even millions, to be able to turn entire populations into robots who would be complete mental slaves . . . should the Russians ever be able to do this, they could very easily enslave the world."

The Death Merchant said nothing, the implication of the terrible weapon stunning him. Should the device ever be perfected and should the Russians use it . . . say from a sub lying off the Eastern Coast of the United States, where close to 1/5th of all Americans live in the 450-mile band that runs from Boston to Washington, D.C.—my God! Over 36,000,000 people would be turned into zombies, into mental and emotional slaves, helpless against the perverted will of their Communist masters . . .

The conclusion was more than obvious: The Mind Blaster was far more dangerous than all the nuclear missiles in the world!

"Richard, I want you to go to Israel and work with the Shin-Bet," Hemms said matter of factly. "We already have top agents in the Middle East area, but I need a man of your experience and know-how. I need you to find that secret Russian base in Egypt and destroy the Mind Blaster. But,"

Hemms paused, "destroying the device is only a part of your job . . ."

A tiny flicker of surprise flared only briefly in the Death Merchant's eyes; then he smiled slightly. "Death is nothing more than the recycling of human beings—but I'm still not anxious to commit suicide. And that's what this mission adds up to, so what more is there?"

"Doctor Yuri Popvikin," Hemms said. "He's a top Russian bio-parapsychologist and physicist and, from what we've heard, the inventor of the Mind Blaster. We think he's there at the Russian job. That's the other half of your job: to kidnap Doctor Popvikin and take him into Israel, after which he'll be secretly flown to the U.S."

Thinking of the almost impossible mission, the Death Merchant shook his head, still smiling, but not speaking. Jacob Hemms continued in his easy manner, "And I know I don't have to tell you that if you're caught . . . we won't know you. You'll be on your own."

"Haven't I always been!" Camellion said drily.

Camellion noticed that Anwar kept glancing at him in the rear-view mirror.

"Just drive," the Death Merchant said softly, "and you might live a bit longer."

Again his thoughts were bitter as he dwelt on his briefing with Hemms. The CIA Director had seriously underestimated the Intelligence arm of the Soviet Union. The GRU had certainly operated with extreme efficiency. He thought of Evers, the double agent! Not only had Soviet Intelligence infiltrated the CIA, but Camellion knew that with the kidnap plot, the GRU had come very close to killing him—and since the Russians were aware of his mission, what else did they know?

The motto over Hemms' desk flashed in his mind! *Yeah, no doubt about it! I'll have to be the meanest son of a bitch in the entire Middle East if I'm to succeed and get out of this alive!*

CHAPTER II

To the casual passer-by, there was nothing unusual about the three-story house on Port Said Street in Cairo, Egypt. Painted white, which caused it to almost glisten in the bright Egyptian sunlight, the stone mansion sat back a hundred feet or so from the road and was surrounded by an ornately grilled fence, perhaps ten feet high, whose double gates were always guarded by two carefully concealed sentries. Several magnificent Cilician firs stood on the well-manicured front lawn.

House and grounds might have been the small estate of some wealthy Egyptian, only they weren't. The Moorish type edifice was the headquarters of Amtorg, the Soviet Union's import-export center in Egypt, a company that also served, on a world-wide basis, as a cover for Russian intelligence.

Ostensibly the director of Amtorg in Cairo was Victor Gulyaiev, an anemic-looking man in his late thirties, with dark hair graying slightly at the temples, and very deep brown eyes. Gulyaiev wore a perpetual smile and most people with whom he came in contact considered him a very friendly man with a surplus of affability, yet his smile was deceptive, for Victor Gulyaiev was a very cruel man, almost as sadistic as his official (to the outside world) "assistant," Constantine Alexis Kagorin, who, as Resident Agent, or chief of the Cairo GRU Residentura, was in reality his boss.

In a second-story room of the Amtorg establishment, two men sat talking. With them was a third GRU agent—Paul Klopkov, a narrow-faced man who, although he was exactly six feet tall, seemed taller because of his slimness. Klopkov, too, had a "legal" cover: he was a correspondent for *Telegrafnoye Agentstvo Sovyetskoyo*, or TASS, as the Soviet news gathering agency is known throughout the world. In reality, Klopkov held the rank of captain in the GRU and had been connected to the Cairo *Apparat* for almost two years.

On this sunny July afternoon, the three men were not the least bit cheerful, especially Colonel Kagorin, who was positively livid with rage, although he didn't reveal his anger by shouting or berating his subordinates. He never displayed his emotions, always speaking calmly and priding himself on his self control.

Colonel Kagorin removed the jeweler's loupe from his eye and, looking up from the table where he had been working on an 18th Century Italian watch, turned to face Klopkov and Gulyaiev. The latter was nervously pacing the floor and smoking a long, cork-tipped Egyptian cigarette, while Klopkov sat by one of the windows, methodically cleaning his finger-nails.

"It's been almost three days," Kagorin said, "and we can make only one safe assumption: the plan to kidnap the Death Merchant failed. Either Boris and Mikhail are dead, or else they're prisoners of the Shin-Bet; otherwise they would have been here by now." He picked up a tiny jeweler's screwdriver, began tapping it on the metal tabletop, and his tone became demanding. "Suggestions as to why *Snegopa* might have failed! Paul, you were in charge of the operation . . ."

Realizing that Kagorin was really giving him a direct order, Klopkov closed the fingernail file and dropped it in his pocket. A member of the dreaded GRU for almost ten years and hence an old experienced pro, Klopkov knew better than to give excuses or to fence around the facts. That would be the wrong procedure with Kagorin.

"I don't know what could have gone wrong, Colonel," Klopkov said simply, his eyes moving to a spot below Kagorin's broad, dark face to the man's open sport shirt, the V of which revealed a tangled mass of dark chest hair. "I am positive that Boris made contact with Camellion. I followed Boris and Camellion onto the jet, pretending I wanted to tell a friend goodbye and I saw Boris seat himself next to the Death Merchant. Possibly something went wrong on the flight between Paris and Tel-Aviv."

"Or after they arrived at Tel-Aviv and after they managed to kidnap the American," Victor Gulyaiev interjected, glancing first at Klopkov, then at Kagorin.

"Or when Boris and Mikhail made the kidnap attempt," Paul said slowly.

Victor gave Paul a hard look. "Well, the plan failed, and since we all know the reputation of this Death Merchant, there's no telling what might have happened! Damn it! This

Camellion is a top international specialist! That's why I suggested drugging him the moment he was in the taxi—and I'm assuming that Boris and Mikhail did manage to get him that far!"

He glared again at Klopkov, who said quickly in irritation, "And I've already explained why I instructed them not to use drugs on the Death Merchant. The plan called for taking Camellion to Station Hg-4 in Jerusalem and then, after he had been smuggled into Amman, Jordan, to fly him here immediately for interrogation. And you, Colonel"—Klopkov turned his attention to Kagorin—"had made it clear that you wanted to question him as soon as possible."

Klopkov turned to Gulyaiev, an angry glow in his eyes. "Do I have to remind you that after a subject is drugged, it takes days before he is rational enough to be questioned, or before truth-inducing drugs, such as pentothal or one of its derivatives, can be used to induce twilight sleep. Besides, Boris and Mikhail were *Mokryye Dela!* They should have been more than able to handle one man, even the Death Merchant!"

Victor Gulyaiev's small mouth twisted wolfishly and, doubling up one fist, he smashed it into the open palm of his other hand. "We could have drugged Camellion and tortured the information out of him after he was flown here!" he said savagely. "No one yet has ever successfully withstood the pain the instruments in the basement can give! This Camellion's only flesh and blood!"

Colonel Kagorin snapped, "Victor, you speak with all the twisted wisdom of a Ukrainian *kolkhozniki!* You've read the thick file on this Camellion! You should know he's not the kind of man who would break under torture, at least not very easily!"

Gulyaiev walked over to the desk and snubbed out his cigarette in a large glass ashtray. "Any man can be broken in time, Colonel," he insisted, lighting another cigarette. He sat down in a wicker easy chair and looked down at the floor, afraid his face might reveal the resentment he harbored for Kagorin. That *Moskva* bastard! Thinking that anyone not born in *Moskva* was a moronic peasant! Well, by God! Having been born in Moscow wouldn't help him when he reported back to The Center in Moscow that the Death Merchant had escaped and that Boris and Mikhail were either dead or in the hands of the damned Jews! Not that

Kagorin wouldn't be able to wriggle out of it. He was a past master at that! He'd merely shift the blame to his subordinates, with special emphasis on Klopkov, and tell General Semichastny, the Director General of the GRU *otdel*, that it was they, not he, who had bungled Operation *Snegopa!* Yes, Kagorin's hands would remain clean from the failure of Operation "Snowfall!"

Victor became further incensed when Kagorin began giving him advice about his personal habits, telling him that he smoked too much.

"Why our own scientists knew years ago, even before the Americans, that the use of tobacco contributes to cancer of the lung and other diseases," Kagorin said calmly. "Instead of placating your nerves with tobacco and alcohol, you should develop a hobby. You might even become an expert on some particular subject. That's how I became an authority on timepieces. Years ago, I developed an interest in clocks and watches. For instance, this watch I'm working on now. The balance wheel is—"

Watching Kagorin and Gulyaiev, Paul Klopkov didn't crack a smile; yet inwardly he laughed, grateful that, at least for the moment, the pressure had been taken off him. Ha! Now Victor had to sit through another "health" lecture!

Klopkov not only despised Kagorin, but Gulyaiev as well, considering them opportunists and feeling that each man was a hypocrite who would stop at nothing to advance himself within the ranks—and this included tossing him to the wolves in the Kremlin. Kagorin in particular, who had far greater mental capabilities than either Klopkov or Gulyaiev! Only Klopkov was aware of this gap in intellect, a cognizance that, in many respects, gave him an advantage over both men, in that he never became personal with them or ever revealed his inner thoughts, no matter how innocuous they might seem. Other agents hadn't been as cautious and circumspect around Colonel Kagorin. There had been Nimov, for instance, who had stupidly asked Kagorin why American workers, since they were supposed to be so oppressed by Capitalists, possessed millions of automobiles. Nimov had been stationed in New York for six months. Two weeks after he asked Kagorin this question, he was recalled to the Soviet Union and shipped to an obscure post near the Mongolian border . . .

Klopkov's wife and two children in Leningrad came first.

Always thinking of them, he never had anything but praise for the men in the Kremlin and their policies.

With an emotionless expression, he watched Kagorin from the corner of his eyes, all the while pretending to toy with a signet ring on his finger and listening to the low steady hum of the air conditioner.

"That's why I don't require such stimulants as tobacco and alcohol to settle my nerves," Kagorin was saying. "I have my watches and clocks to occupy my free time, and by keeping my emotions under control, I am able to give my very best to Mother Russia."

He shook a finger at Gulyaiev and Klopkov. "You both should keep that in mind: giving all your talents to the Communist cause."

Kagorin's tone was fatherly, as though the other two men were little boys and he far older and wiser than they, although he was only in his middle forties . . . a few years older than Klopkov.

He was a heavy man, this Constantine Alexis Kagorin, a slow moving man of medium height and solidly built, the pounds packed until they added up to 231. A ruggedly handsome man, too . . . Perhaps it was his many freckles that gave to his face an illusion of youth. Not only did they cover the bridge of his nose, but most of his face as well. His hair was black, slightly wavy and half-curled in the back —so heavy that it detracted from his inky eyes, which were small, yet piercing.

Victor Gulyaiev looked thoughtfully at his cigarette. "I do have a hobby, Alexis," he said nonchalantly. "My work. You see, I do give everything I've got to the cause and to Mother Russia, just as you do."

Realizing that he couldn't argue with Victor's logic, Kagorin didn't immediately comment. Instead, he picked up the jeweler's loupe and returned to the business at hand. He carefully avoided looking directly at Gulyaiev.

"Tomorrow, we'll recall Merkulov from Paris," he said evenly. "An agent of Camellion's caliber is always extremely perceptive. No doubt he'll put two and two together, as the Americans say, and arrive at the answer that it was Josef who fingered him for Boris and Mikhail. It's a pity that Merkulov will have to break his cover as 'John Cecil Evers,' but it can't be helped. I can't take the chance of losing him. And should the CIA get to him first . . ."

23

Paul Klopkov said, "I could go to Jerusalem and personally investigate the Camellion matter. Our Apparat there should have some word. Either our men arrived at the station or they did not—with or without the Death Merchant!"

"Absolutely not," Kagorin said quickly, fingering one end of his small mustache. "You're too valuable a man and you also know the location of the Psychotron base. Anyhow, the third day will be up tonight at 10:30, and then the Jerusalem Apparat will contact us. We'll know then what went wrong with Snegopa! At least we'll know if Boris and Mikhail got there—or else the Apparat won't have any information, in which case we'll have to turn assumptions into facts and proceed from there."

"If the Death Merchant's alive?" Victor asked. He removed his tinted glasses and began wiping the lenses with a large silk handkerchief.

Paul Klopkov offered, "I still am of the opinion that we should have the Apparat in Jerusalem make radio contact every other day. Every third day forces us to do too much catching up when some emergency occurs. The Israeli monitoring service isn't that damn good!"

"The Shin-Bet is every bit that good!" Kagorin said rather sharply. "That's why even every third day is risky. But to lengthen the contact beyond that would seriously put us at a disadvantage. That is not the problem now. Richard Camellion is. It's just too damn bad he's not on our side."

"But he's only one man!" Victor insisted. He had risen and was pouring himself a glass of iced peppermint tea.

Kagorin's eyes narrowed and he said, "Unlike you, Victor, I am not going to underestimate the capabilities of this man. Merkulov had made it more than clear what the Death Merchant's mission is: to find and destroy the Psychotron base and kidnap Doctor Popvikin! Can you imagine the nerve of the man, thinking he might even possibly do either one! But that's precisely what makes him so dangerous—his very audacity!"

Klopkov spoke up. "He can't possibly succeed!" He felt Colonel Kagorin was imparting too much talent to the Death Merchant, but did not say so.

"Nevertheless, I consider the Death Merchant the most dangerous man to our cause in the entire Middle East!" Kagorin said flatly. "You ask, Victor, our course of action should we learn that Camellion is still alive. I'm asking The Center to send SMERSH specialists to help us kill Camellion.

If he is in Israel, it will be their task to find and kill him." Pausing, he stroked his mustache again, then began twirling the loupe on his finger. "Keep this in mind, though: our main job is to protect Dr. Popvikin and his staff and to see that the final Psychotron experiments are conducted on schedule."

"Granted that the Death Merchant is an extremely clever and dangerous man," Paul Klopkov said, "I still doubt that he'd have the time to do much of anything. Dr. Popvikin has succeeded in increasing the range of the machine, and once—"

"I know that!" Kagorin said irritably, cutting him short. "As soon as Popvikin is ready, the device will be tested on Bir El Tamadeh. In the meantime—Victor, send a dozen more agents to the base, or should I say 'Meteorological technicians?' The more security Popvikin and his technicians have, the better I'll feel about it."

Klopkov got up and went over to the tea set on the shesham table. He said, "I for one fail to see how the Death Merchant could even find the base, much less manage to get to Dr. Popvikin. The base is too well camouflaged for the Israelis to discover it by aerial reconnaissance, and from the ground, even if they should manage to get an agent into the area, what could he learn? Even the Egyptians think it's a meteorological station!"

He finished pouring the tea into a tall glass, and again sat down, this time by the library table, on which rested a chess set, the pieces made of ivory, the board of inlaid mahogany.

"The Germans have a saying that for someone full of hope the sky is strung with violins," Kagorin said crossly, his beady little eyes knifing at Klopkov. "But there's a difference between hope and over-confidence—remember that!"

The Russian Colonel seemed to be completely at ease, almost completely relaxed. The hard glance vanished from his eyes and the thick lips crooked into a half-smile. The thought came to Gulyaiev, who was looking at his chief, that the freckles across the bridge of his nose were suddenly standing out like tiny spots glued to the skin, no longer part of the flesh.

Scratching his chin, Gulyaiev decided to interject some levity into the conference, saying quickly, "You know, Alexis, if I were you, I wouldn't even bother to call in the SMERSH boys. In only a very short while, Popvikin will have perfected the Psychotron, and then we'll have the secret of telepathic

25

hypnosis. All we'll have to do is beam in on Israel and turn all these damned Jews into robots, including Camellion!"

When he saw the disapproving look flare up in Kagorin's eyes, Gulyaiev realized that his humor was not being appreciated and became silent, taking a long time to open a new pack of cigarettes. The hell with Alexis and his "advice!" Let him play with his damn clocks and watches!

Kagorin's voice was flat and deadly. "Victor, you know as well as I do that the Soviet Union isn't about to use the Psychotron to help these foolish Egyptians in their so called 'Holy War' against the Jews. Once Dr. Popvikin has concluded his experiments, the complex out in the desert will be dismantled and the device taken to Moscow for complete evaluation—and I don't intend to let anyone or anything interfere with those experiments, including that damned Death Merchant!" He thought of the spy cell in Jerusalem. But none of the agents there knew the location of the Psychotron base, nor did Boris and Mikhail—fortunately.

Smirking, Paul Klopkov said, "At least we don't have to worry about the Egyptians and their so called 'secret service!' " He sipped at this tea. "Those fellows couldn't find the Pyramids in a one acre park!"

"I wish we could say the same thing for that fat fool Assad," Gulyaiev said, laughing slightly. "It's a good thing he doesn't know what we're really doing near Suez!"

Colonel Kagorin leaned back in his swivel chair, and its back shook slightly under the sudden pressure. "Speaking of our 'dear friend,' Hasan El Assad," he mused in a mocking voice, "we had no choice but to let him know about the complex. As Minister of the Interior of the United Arab Republic, he would have eventually discovered the base and perhaps have created a real stink, one that might have reached the ears of Shin-Bet agents. As it turned out, somehow they learned about it anyhow, but not until after we destroyed Bel Sida. However, we need not concern ourselves with Assad. Since Bel Sida, he knows we're experimenting with something, but we've convinced him that the Psychotron base is nothing more than a meteorological station. By the time he finds out the truth, if ever, we'll have the device back in the Soviet Union."

Once more Kagorin placed the loupe in his eye and returned his attention to the work table, on whose surface lay clustered the various parts of a large pocket watch. With

26

tweezers, he carefully picked up the escape wheel and, putting its axial in the hub of the balance wheel, which he held steady with another pair of tweezers, he pushed the upper half of its rachets into the grooves of the crown wheel. Pleased with his progress, Kagorin inspected the detail of each piece. Ahhhh, exactly right. Those old Italian craftsmen! Such artists they were! Hmmmmm . . . but the pallet! An odd fit indeed!

Almost tenderly, Kagorin lifted the 3-wheel combination, which he had just assembled, and put them into the gold, highly ornamented case.

"Paul," he said, pausing as he barely touched the side of the crown wheel with a Menten pick. "Paul, I want you to make arrangements to transfer our Apparat in Jerusalem. Boris and Mikhail know its location, and if they are in the hands of the Jews, if they should talk . . ." *Ahhh, now for the mainspring!*

Kagorin felt that Klopkov had already made arrangements for the transfer, realizing that his third-in-command, as thorough as he was, was also aware of the danger that confronted the GRU cell in the Holy Land. *There! The wheel is balanced. That pallet worries me though . . .*

Paul Klopkov said, "Even if Boris and Mikhail were taken, it will be a day or so before the Israelis can break them down with truth drugs; and their psychological pre-conditioning to interrogation was the best. But," and he shrugged, "this is the third day . . ."

"That isn't what Alexis said!" Victor snapped. "He said—"

"I've already made plans for the removal of the Apparat from Jerusalem," Paul said calmly, ignoring him. "We must, however, be prepared for the worst. If we receive no word tonight from them . . . well, then it will be obvious that Boris and Mikhail have talked and that the Jerusalem cell has been taken."

"The new locale?" Kagorin asked. Leaning closer, he peered through the loupe and gingerly tapped at the balance wheel.

Paul put his glass on the floor beside him. "Amman in Jordan is our only choice," he explained seriously. "We have only seven agents in the Jerusalem cell, and they can be assimilated into the Amman unit. Of course, the change will make contact with our agents in Tel-Aviv more difficult, but at the same time will not interfere with our network in Syria or Iraq."

Victor Gulyaiev blew a tiny cloud of blue smoke into the

27

air and began rubbing his chin. "What about the special test in Jerusalem?" he asked. "Schedule B., as it stands now, calls for our cell there to use a portable Psychotron in the local area, provided Popvikin can build one in time."

"We'll know more about that after tonight, if our cell makes radio contact," Kagorin said, not looking up. A thin twist of a smile crossed his lips, both because he had succeeded with the balance wheel and because he appreciated efficiency in his men—and that's what it would take to eliminate the Death Merchant: extreme efficiency.

A slow and deadly hatred for Richard Camellion began burning in Alexis Kagorin's mind. He had so wanted the American swine captured and flown to Cairo—and it wouldn't have required pentothal or penzocaine to make him talk! Definitely not! The instruments in the basement, deep underneath the house, would have been just as effective, and the question and answer session would have been more pleasurable.

Kagorin's jaw muscles began twitching!

One way or another, I'll still get to hear the Death Merchant beg and scream for mercy!

CHAPTER III

With a monotonous rotation, the blades of the ceiling fan turned slowly, like the lazy arms of a windmill that had been turned to a horizontal position—not that the Israeli Intelligence Service couldn't afford an air conditioner for this particular headquarters conference room. The reason for the fan was simple enough. Sudden, abrupt changes of temperature—and this is what happens when one leaves an air conditioned building and goes out into the summer sunshine—are not conducive to adjusting oneself to the climate of the Middle East; and if one is very active physically and moves about the countryside, it is only sensible to forego momentary comfort in preference for a gradual acclimation, which is insurance against a sudden heat-stroke. In July, it is very hot in the little nation of Israel.

However, the four men sitting around the table appeared to be comfortable enough. Richard Camellion was certainly relaxed, his face entirely free of perspiration. Sitting at one end of the table, the Death Merchant faced Isser Lev Langbein, the Israeli-born Chief of the Shin-Bet.

A large jowled man in his early sixties, quick moving and fast speaking, Langbein had been a leader in the Haganah, the Jewish Defense Force in Palestine which later, after independence, formed the nucleus of the Israeli Army.

Next to the Shin-Bet chief, to his left, sat one of the best operatives in the Israeli Intelligence Service—Ethan Friedenthal, a tall, cadaverous-looking man, not quite fifty; a sad-eyed man whose dreams were often filled with the acid of bitter memories, with wild nightmares revolving around his youth in Hitler's Germany and a hell-on-earth called Auschwitz. The barbed wire would cut into his brain. He would hear the hideous screams of the doomed and smell the sweet stench of burning flesh . . . But some nights Friedenthal's sleep was peaceful and undisturbed. Some nights he even smiled in his sleep! For Friedenthal was one of the Shin-Bet agents who had successfully tracked Adolf Eichmann and brought the infamous Nazi murderer to justice.

29

An expensively dressed, athletic type man, wearing a peacock colored sportscoat, was on Langbein's right. A handsome man in his early thirties, with carefully combed blond hair and features that bordered on "pretty," Gordon Lyle Norstead was a CIA "contact" agent and information analyst. For a cover, he posed as a wisecracking, hard-drinking American playboy, the result being that Gordon—usually with a beautiful parasite on each arm—was a well-known figure in Tel-Aviv night spots and on the resort beaches along the Mediterranean coast; he was no stranger to the night life in Beirut, Lebanon; in Damascus, Syria and in Bagdad, Iraq.

Norstead was not in a joking mood as he said, "In my opinion, the situation is on the brink of being calamitous. This latest piece of intelligence that the Soviets have a cell operating in Jerusalem—and a *Mokryye Dela* unit at that—complicates the entire situation." He gave Camellion a long, admiring look. "I'm still wondering how you managed to escape from those two Russians who tried to put the snatch on you! They were the best—or don't you know what *Mokryye Dela* means in Russian?"

Camellion shrugged and glanced at his wrist watch. "I had no choice," he said simply. "I wasn't in the mood to die. *Mokryye Dela?* I believe the phrase refers to the GRU's 'Department of Wet Affairs.' "

"The phrase means exactly that," Ethan Friedenthal said solemnly, without looking up from the shiny surface of the table. "Literally translated, *'Mokryye'* means 'wet,' and in this case it means 'blood wet'—terror and assassination!"

"Which means we can be positive of one thing," Langbein said. "The Russian agents in the Holy City are there, probably, for purposes of mass murder!"

"If they're actually in Jerusalem!" Friedenthal said. He turned and looked directly at Langbein. "That's the catch—can we believe the captured Russian agent?"

"Do we have a choice?" Norstead asked.

Camellion said lazily, "This is my third day in Israel and I consider those three days wasted. We haven't been moving fast enough to suit me."

Langbein spread his hands before him in a gesture of helplessness. "We've had no choice, Camellion," he said somewhat crossly. "You smashed in the teeth of that Russian and the medication we had to give him interfered with the effectiveness of the sodium pentothal. We were lucky that he talked at all!"

Camellion put his arms on the arms of the chair, folded his hands in his lap and began turning his thumbs around each other. "I am well aware of that fact," he agreed. "But we've still lost three days; that's why I'm in favor of raiding the shop in Jerusalem as soon as possible. I know from past experience that Colonel Kagorin is an extremely cautious man. The moment he learns that the kidnap plot failed and that one of his agents has been taken, he is going to dissolve the Jerusalem Apparat—and we'll be left with a handful of nothing!"

Ethan Friedenthal moved his gaze in Camellion's direction. "You're assuming the Russian you captured is telling the truth," he insisted. "Actually, we don't know that a Russian cell is operating in the Holy City."

"Nor will we ever know, if we keep sitting here talking about it!" the Death Merchant countered. "Those 'blood wet' boys are probably moving right now!"

Friedenthal did not reply. He stole a quick glance at Camellion, feeling secretly guilty because, although he had not met the Death Merchant until a few days ago, he felt a strong antipathy toward the man. Why, he did not know. Because Camellion reminded him of an SS officer he had once known in Auschwitz? Perhaps that was the answer . . .

"The Russian agent couldn't have lied," Langbein said. "Even though he was probably pre-conditioned for questioning, he had enough pentothal in him to make even a pathological liar tell the truth. And, five different times he told the same story. I'm confident he told the truth." His eyes went to Camellion, then fastened on Gordon Norstead. "Don't you agree?"

Norstead nodded, and Richard Camellion said, "I think we can say with a large measure of certainty that Russian agents are operating in the Christian Quarter of Jerusalem and that—"

"You have to give those Red bastards credit!" Norstead said with a low chuckle. "Imagine! Using a Roman Catholic shop for tourists as a cover!"

"And that the sooner we hit them, the better!" Camellion concluded.

"The shop should be under surveillance by now," Isser Langbein said quickly. "I'd prefer watching the place for a few days because it's possible we could find the source of some of their contacts throughout the Middle East, but we haven't the time. I know that."

"We'd have to trail every tourist that goes into the shop," Ethan said.

"We'll know more about the situation as soon as Jock gets back and reports on the arrangements he's made with Israela and her group," Langbein explained. "You've never met her, Camellion. She's head of our Intelligence section in Jerusalem—and very capable she is, too."

The Death Merchant leaned forward, putting his arms on the table. "All of you seem to be forgetting the time factor involved," he pointed out. "Quite obviously those foreign agents in the Holy City are wondering what went wrong with the kidnap plot, why Boris and Mikhail and I haven't shown up at the Catholic Shop!"

No one said anything, and Camellion continued. "The moment they learn Mikhail's been taken, they're going to move. They probably have a once or twice-a-week contact with Kagorin in Cairo, and once they report to him that the kidnap plot failed, he's going to tell them to move and go into 'deepest black'—but fast. I say: raid the place right now. Hit the Catholic Shop with everything we've got!"

"I agree with you, Richard," Norstead said very seriously, "but I doubt if any of the Russians in the Jerusalem Apparat know the location of the Mind Blaster base in Egypt." He finished lighting a small cigar. "Colonel Kagorin's not going to trust such precious information to men in the field."

"You took care of the Evers' matter?" Camellion asked Norstead.

A thin curl of blue-gray smoke drifted upward from Norstead's nostrils. He looked at Camellion's calm, intelligent face and nodded slowly. "We'll try to take the son of a bitch alive, but don't count on it. He probably went into hiding and will remain there until he learns whether or not the kidnap plot succeeded."

The Death Merchant's eyes bored into the tired face of Isser Lev Langbein. "Well, are we going to continue to sit here, or do we raid the Catholic Shop?"

"We wait until Jock reports in!" Langbein said, his voice rising in anger. "And let me remind you, Camellion, your orders are to work with us, not to make policy. I'd appreciate your remembering that!"

"My orders are to find the Psychotron base in Egypt and to kidnap Doctor Popvikin!" Camellion snapped. "I can't accomplish either one by sitting here in Shin-Bet headquarters. And you remember something: I always complete my missions!"

Disgusted with the entire business and feeling that Langbein was being too cautious, Camellion looked toward the single window at the end of the small room. Dusk was settling like a dark blanket, and in the distance he could see the Shalom Mayer Tower, Tel-Aviv's leading department store.

Another thing that troubled him was the possibility that he might have to work with this Israela. Women were so damned undependable! On the other hand, since she was the leader of a Shin-Bet unit, she had to be a very unusual, if not an astonishing, woman. She was a Sabra, which meant she had probably spent several years in the Israeli Army and was no stranger to violence. Nevertheless, the Death Merchant was worried—*I'm not any closer to finding the Psychotron base than I was three days ago! And all we do is sit here and talk* . . .

"It's more or less a calculated gamble," Langbein said in a more friendly tone, "but as soon as Jock reports in, I'll decide what course of action to take. I'd prefer to develop intelligence on the kind of trouble the Russians are supposed to stir up . . . before we move in on them. Any kind of trouble in the Holy City wouldn't be good for Jewish morale."

Friedenthal said slowly, "According to our Russian friend, the Apparat in the Holy City is tied in with the Mind Blaster. If only we knew exactly how."

"All the more reason to raid the Catholic Shop as soon as possible," the Death Merchant reminded the men at the table. "Or it's just possible that the people in Jerusalem might be deprived of their sanity! Stop and think of the possibilities! Suppose the Russians have already succeeded in increasing the range of the Psychotron? It's not inconceivable that Popvikin's developed a portable model!"

Langbein was about to speak when a small buzzer, underneath the table, announced that someone wanted to enter the conference room. Langbein pressed a button, unlocking the electrically-controlled door, and Eddie "Jock" Heydecker walked into the room.

A short, wiry individual in his early forties. Heydecker had been a Captain in the British Army, giving up his British

33

citizenship and emigrating to Israel in 1961. A weapons system expert, Jock was a friendly man, almost completely bald and with two lower front teeth missing. He was also fond of saying that he was the only Jew in Israel with a Cockney accent (which he wasn't).

Sitting down at the table, next to Norstead, Jock quickly made his report. Yes, he had discussed the situation with Israela, and they had set up a surveillance schedule around the Catholic Shop of St. Francis Way— ". . . as much as we could!" Jock concluded.

The Death Merchant gave Jock a searching look. "What do you mean—as much as you could? Or are you saying the location of the place makes surveillance difficult?"

"That's it, matey!" Jock replied almost jovially, speaking as though he were discussing plans for a party. "You see, St. Francis is a narrow street, narrow and winding. We can't station agents across from the shop or they'd be as conspicuous as ink spots on white paper. What we're doing is having our people saunter past the shop disguised as tourists and Arabs. As for the back entrance—it's impossible to station agents without making them look like sore thumbs. Those Russian chaps would spot our boys immediately."

The Death Merchant gazed at Isser Lev Langbein, calmly and unemotionally. Pushing back his chair, he stood up and, reaching into his coat, adjusted the heavy S. & W. Magnums in their specially made shoulder holsters.

"Victory has a hundred fathers," he said, "but failure is always an orphan." He glanced through the window at the darkness. "We have no choice but to raid the Catholic Shop and we'd better do it before the sun comes up tomorrow morning!"

"Or those GRU chaps in Jerusalem might not be there!" Jock Heydecker said. He leaned back, tipping the back legs of the wooden chair, and pushed his tongue through the opening made by his missing teeth. Then he said, "I say throw a cordon around the shop and bag the lot of them!"

The Chief of the Israel Secret Service pushed back his chair, stood up, and addressed himself to the Death Merchant. "You're right, Camellion. You and I and Jock will fly immediately to the Holy City. Ethan, you remain here as liaison officer. Norstead?" Langbein's eyes searched Gordon's handsome face.

"Count me out," Gordon said emphatically. "There's no

34

point in risking my cover unnecessarily. I don't want to be seen with you fellows. But I wish I could go! When I stop to think of all the booze I have to guzzle as part of my role— I'll be lucky if I don't eventually develop cirrhosis of the liver!"

"But think of the fun you have, matey!" Jock laughed.

Norstead lit another cigar, and turned toward the Death Merchant. "You're a man who's supposed to have all the answers, Richard," he said, grinning. "How would you handle my job and still protect your health?"

Norstead spoke in a joking manner, but Camellion detected a note of urgency in the man's voice and felt he was actually seeking advice.

The Death Merchant smiled and said, "I couldn't handle your cover. I've a nervous stomach and don't drink."

Jock Heydecker's mouth almost fell open, and he stared curiously at the Death Merchant, wondering what made the killing machine tick. There he stood, a slim chap, looking like a college professor about to give a lecture . . . a man who had probably been in a thousand gun battles and had killed as many people, perhaps more. Why damn it! The bloody bloke was even more of a weirdo than they said he was!

Suddenly, Jock felt very sorry for the Russian agents in Jerusalem!

God help them when they confronted the Death Merchant . . .

CHAPTER IV

Anxious to transform Israela's face and his own, Richard Camellion leaned closer and studied the girl's facial structure. Not what he had expected, she was a very attractive young woman. Her soft hair—as black as raven's feathers—curled at the ends but otherwise fell straight and shiny around her face. It was a vital face, a bit thin and pale but beautifully shaped, the sable eyes made large and somewhat doll-like by the long dark lashes. She had a finely shaped, slightly tilted nose and very even teeth. Her mouth was a bit too large, but it was a generous full mouth with a dimple in the right corner. The rest of her was built to match: breasts that were full and rounded, seemingly struggling for release against the thin cotton material of her blouse, a slim waist, nice hips, long, deeply tanned legs.

Richard got the impression that she was the kind of girl who, had she been an American woman, would have a preference for black lace lingerie.

"Do you have a last name or were your parents stingy?" he asked, turning to the card table on which a large metal suitcase lay opened, its contents revealing a complete theatrical makeup kit. There were powders and paints, various creams and tintshades; nose putty, beards, mustaches and numerous wigs, even feminine ones, in case the Death Merchant wanted to effect the disguise of a woman; a dozen or so specially made latex rubber face masks. A hundred different "characters" lay in the suitcase, and Richard Camellion, at one time or another, had used every one of them.

"Diamant," Israela said matter of factly, looking into his eyes, knowing he was seeing her only as a face and not as a woman, perhaps not even as a person! "My last name is Diamant." She sat on a folding chair to one side of the card table, and as Camellion, who was sitting in front of her, put his finger lightly on her cheek, tracing the cheek bone, she asked, "I'm curious, Death Merchant. Why did—"

"I'd prefer you didn't call me that!" Camellion said sharply. He reached into the suitcase and picked up a gray-white feminine wig and a face mask. "The term implies I 'sell' death."

Adjusting the lamp so that the light focused directly on the girl's face, he wondered why the Shin-Bet couldn't have had better lighting in its Jerusalem headquarters. And the overhead fluorescent light wouldn't do at all.

"Don't you?" Israela asked, her tone slightly sarcastic. Watching him closely—she had heard so many stories about this legendary man—she saw not a flicker of emotion cross his somewhat boyish face. She decided then that he wasn't a bad looking man. No . . . not bad-looking, but far from handsome. He did have a pleasant face, with eyes that were very blue, but sad, as though he had seen too much misery and suffering for one man and perhaps he had . . . Closely cropped dark brown hair—and he wasn't a large man. Not quite six feet tall, he was muscular, weighing, oh, perhaps 170 pounds. But was he really a human killing machine?

"What were you about to ask—why did I what?" Camellion said. He cupped his fingers around her chin and pushed her head back slightly. "And hold still. It's almost nine o'clock and we don't have too much time."

"Why did you make the others leave the room?" Israela asked. "Do people make you nervous when they watch you work as a makeup artist?"

"Nervous, no. Bore me with silly questions, yes. Now be quiet while I slip this mask over your face."

Israela smiled. "Yes, master."

As he worked, adding years to the girl's face, transforming the smooth clear skin into the wrinkled face of a woman in her middle sixties, the Death Merchant analyzed the plan that he and Langbein and Jock had evolved while flying to Jerusalem in an IAF helicopter. They had agreed that it was essential to approach the Catholic Shop surreptitiously; that they capture, for questioning, as many Russian agents as possible; and—as Langbein had insisted—do the latter with a minimum of effort, which meant with very little violence.

Camellion had not commented, having already decided to do the job his own way.

Jock told Langbein, "You're asking the impossible, Chief. Those Russian blighters will never surrender. Our best bet is to smother the shop with a lot of fire power and hope for the best."

It was the Death Merchant who had arrived at a ready

37

solution: He and Israela, if she were willing, would enter the shop disguised as tourists and take the Russians by surprise—in disguise because Israela was a well known Shin-Bet agent, and because, in all probability, the Russians had the DM's photograph in order to identify him to their "legals" and "illegals" in the Middle East.

The attack of Camellion and Israela would be synchronized with a two-pronged spearhead by the Israeli Security Police who would rush both the front and back entrances of the Catholic Shop. The trap would be closed, hopefully, on at least two or three Russian intelligence agents. With forceful persuasion, they might provide some clue to the location of the Mind Blaster base in Egypt.

With a soft brush the Death Merchant began "paling" Israela's lips, while he analyzed the coming raid. He didn't find it the least bit fantastic that Russian Intelligence should have an *Apparat* operating within Jerusalem's Temple Area, part of whose ancient walls contained the famous Wailing Wall, the latter of which was larger and heavier than the other walls, but shorter in length.

Camellion thought of this Wailing Wall, knowing that it was this relic, more than anything else, that told the Jews they were living in the City of God. No other site in the world, so said the Jews, had absorbed so much agony; no monument had ever given a people such collective strength, which is why the Jews were able to say: *We are surrounded by millions of Arabs, but we have no fear . . .*

A voice of caution whispered within the Death Merchant's brain, quietly telling him that the Catholic Shop would not be easy to take, that the possibilities for the escape of the Russian agents were numerous. Suppose they blew up the place? The way the Temple Area was laid out! The streets were narrow as alleys, and they twisted and climbed. Some were covered and looked like tunnels. There were all manner of steep passages and declivities.

Richard knew that an old friend would be with him and Israela every second—DEATH!

Glancing quickly at his watch—almost 9:30—Camellion inspected his handiwork. The attractive twenty-five-year-old girl had vanished, and now in her place sat an elderly woman

38

with gray-white hair, whose cheeks were pale and wrinkled, the whole face sagging with age.

Satisfied that he had done a good job, Richard picked up a round mirror from the table and handed it to the girl, delighting in her examination of surprise.

"Why it's almost impossible to believe!" Israela gasped. "It's —it's not me!" As if trying to regain her true identity, she touched her fingertips to her face . . . almost fearfully.

Without commenting, the Death Merchant began working on his own disguise. He picked up a gray wig from the suitcase and expertly slipped it over his head, after which he fastened down the edges with spirit gum. Then he began fashioning putty to reshape his mouth and nose.

A short time later, Israela's "husband" had been created: an old man who could have been in his early seventies. Getting to his feet and hunching over, the old boy cackled, his words broken with age, "Well my dear . . . shall we go?"

Ten minutes later, after changing clothes, the "elderly" American tourists were in the back seat of a Volvo, riding from the Shin-Bet station, close to the Central Post Office, along Koresh St.

"We'll turn on Shlomo Hamelech, go down Hativat Hatzanhanim, and enter the Temple Area via the New Gate entrance," Jock, who was driving, called back.

Sitting next to him, the Chief of the Shin-Bet said, "St. Francis Way is only a short distance from the New Gate Road. We'll let the two of you off close to the Holy Sepulchre and you can walk the rest of the way. You won't have any trouble getting there, Camellion. Israela is well acquainted with the area."

They proceeded in silence, Camellion's eyes missing nothing. He noticed Hebrew and Arab newspapers being sold from the same stand.

The Volvo passed a sign: American Cigarettes ninety cents a pack.

Tiny stalls selling a favorite tidbit, round rolls encrusted with sesame seeds and served with a hard-boiled egg. They passed stalls selling *gazoz*, a raspberry-flavored carbonated water; open sheds displaying trays of *felafel*, a kind of vegetarian meatball made of chicken-peas and peppers; and neat occidental posters advertising—of all things—Ponds

Almond Cream atop dried figs, miniature apricots, almonds from the other side of the Jordan, mysterious-looking herbs from India . . . walnuts, vine leaves, and bright orange-colored lentils.

Twenty-one minutes later the Death Merchant and Israela Diamant were ambling along St. Francis Way, both dressed as American tourists, Camellion in an old fashioned blue suit of summer weight, Israela wearing a printed cotton dress, flat-heeled shoes, and carrying a large shopping bag in which rested an Israeli-made UZI sub-machine gun and other items, underneath a few dummy packages.

They were ignored by people brushing past them . . . by Jews . . . by Arabs wearing the kaffyeh, or white headdress bound with black ropes (some of them dressed as Westerners, whiles others wore the traditional burnoose, a hooded mantle or cloak) and by tourists from a dozen different nations.

Noticing that a lot of the men were dressed in plain white shirts, Camellion asked Israela the reason, and she told him that "a white shirt, open at the neck, might be called the national costume of Israel, at least for the men." She added, "A necktie salesman would starve to death in Jerusalem."

Then, finally, they were approaching the open, but narrow, doorway of the Catholic Shop, the front of which was stone and whose window displayed religious articles of Roman Catholicism. There were holy medals and medallions; statues of Christ and His mother, of the Holy Family, of the Apostles, of the various saints; beautiful lithographed prints; candles and Crucifixes; tiny bottles of holy water; round vials containing soil from the Mount of Olives.

Leaning heavily on his cane (one would have thought the old man was about to topple over!) Camellion whispered, "Don't take any chances, Israela, but move when I do." Privately, he felt she would fall apart when the action started, but he kept his thoughts to himself.

They walked into the dimly lighted shop, passing a young couple just leaving.

A sullen-faced young man, whose head was shaven and who was wearing a white clerk's coat, was behind one counter. An older man, also wearing a white coat, sat behind the opposite counter, while at the back of the shop a pinch-faced flat-chested woman was arranging candlesticks. She reminded Camellion of a spinster from some Victorian novel. She

40

glanced up as the old couple shuffled into the store, then returned to her work.

Perhaps a few year older than Israela, the dour-looking clerk was brusque to the point of rudeness. "You'll have to hurry," he said without the least trace of an accent. "We're closing for the night."

Instantly, the Death Merchant analyzed the setup, a desperate plan forming in his agile mind. Close to where no-tits was working, in the back of the room, a heavy curtain hung in a large arched doorway. Hmmmm, the entrance to a back room. And beyond that room?

"Didn't you hear me, old man?" the clerk asked crossly. "I said we're closing for the day."

With pseudo timidity, the old man stepped up to the counter and cackled, "Me and my Missus here, we're interested in a statue of Saint Joseph, young feller. Like the kind on the shelf there."

With the tip of his cane he pointed to a foot high statue on the shelf behind the clerk, who then turned, picked up the statue, and placed it on the counter.

The old tourist turned to his wife. "Is this the one you wanted, dear?" he asked. "Yes, sir, it sure would look good on our dresser."

Not being able to disguise her voice, Israela merely nodded. "The price is one Israeli pound," the clerk said in a bored voice.

Picking up the St. Joseph statue, Camellion pretended to study it, turning slightly, his movement giving him an opportunity to glance in the direction of the other clerk who was behind the opposite counter. Short, heavyset and uglier than an over-worked prostitute on a Sunday morning, the man had gotten up and was leaning against the shelves, his arms folded across his chest. He was gazing in Camellion's direction.

The old codger turned to Israela and looked deep into her eyes, saying in the voice of a man in the icy years of life, "Check your souvenirs, Mother, and we'll put this here statue in the bag."

Nodding, Israela bent down and began fumbling with the shopping bag, glancing up every now and then at her "husband."

Turning back to the clerk, the old man smiled. "Uh huh, a fine statue. Guess we'll take it, young man. You needn't wrap it."

"One pound," the clerk said.

Nonchalantly, as though reaching for his billfold, Camellion put his hand inside his coat—and then he exploded into action! He pulled the hand out of the suit coat, only it contained a fistful of .357 Magnum. Before the clerk's thought processes had time to tell him what was happening, the Death Merchant slammed the 6" barrel against his right temple, sending him into dreamland as dexterously as a butcher poleaxes a bull in a slaughter house. As though his legs had suddenly turned to soft wax, the Russian agent began melting to the floor, even as the Death Merchant jumped to one side, shoving Israela in the process. His movements saved their lives, because the Russian across the room was extremely fast. The Death Merchant figured he would be. As highly trained as they were, the Soviet Union's "blood wet affair" boys always reacted with lightning speed.

The Russian agent jerked out a Gorlenski machine pistol from underneath the counter and triggered off a stream of fire toward where Camellion and Israela had been standing. The machine pistol sounded like a runaway typewriter as a line of hot steel sliced across the room and found a home behind the counter, sizzling in a row of St. Joseph statues and a row of Madonna figurines and exploding them into chunks of useless plaster-of-Paris!

In the back of the shop, the prune-faced Russian bitch yelled a warning in Russian to whoever was in the back room and, reaching into a large urn, came up with another machine pistol; but the Death Merchant's sudden action had taken her completely by surprise and she reacted more slowly than the agent behind the counter. She was swinging the twelve-inch barrel toward the old folks when one of the Death Merchant's Magnums roared and a heavy slug sang its sad song of death, catching the GRU jerk above the bridge of the nose and blowing apart a billion brain cells. Before he had time to think, the Russian intelligence officer, whose name was Gregory Benzeikovavitch, found himself in the middle of Hell, sitting stupidly on Stalin's hot lap. Amid a shower of shattered skull bone, scattered brains and bright blood, one of the Kremlin's best sank to the floor.

Almost but not quite as quick as the Death Merchant, Israela had pulled her UZI machine gun from the shopping bag, and while the Russian woman was leveling down on Camellion, Israela cured all her earthly problems with a short

42

burst of slugs that hit Vera Istenova squarely in her skinny breasts, the blast of hot steel knocking her backwards through the heavy red curtain that divided the shop proper from the back room.

Practically cut in two by the dozen or so slugs and with the curtain half-wrapped around her like a flowing shroud, Vera Istenova wilted to the floor, pulling the curtain down with her.

Crouching low, the Death Merchant whispered fiercely to Israela, who continued to hold her UZI ready, "Get down behind that counter. I'll take the left, and we'll work our way toward the back. Keep down until I make a move—understand!"

Nodding quickly, her face grim, Israela jumped behind the counter, and Camellion, with the pungent odor of cordite stinging his nostrils, got down behind the opposite counter and began crawling toward the back room. The Russian he had knocked out lay there like a log, a bloody gash on his temple—*I hope I didn't kill the slob!* He felt the Russian's pulse. *Yeah, the Lenin lover is still alive, but he's probably got a fractured skull. He'll live long enough to be questioned—and executed or exchanged.* Camellion also felt better about Israela, admitting to himself that he had misjudged her. She was more than level-headed under fire: she was deadly.

Smiling thinly and with the melody of *La Donna é mobile* running through his mind, the Death Merchant reached the end of the protective counter. Six feet away, a bit to his right, was the arched entrance to the back room. Very cautiously he peeked around the corner of the counter. The Russian hag was lying on her back, torrents of blood pouring from her chest onto the floor.

Seeing Israela peeping around the corner of her wooden counter, Richard indicated that he wanted her to fire a burst at the top of the entrance, also telling her with hand motions that he would rush the room while she prevented its occupants, if any, from rushing them. She winked and pointed the barrel of the UZI upward.

Police whistles from outside! The Israeli police were getting ready to rush the Catholic Shop!

Tensing himself, Camellion gave Israela the go-ahead sign, and she opened fire, the slugs stabbing into the back room, a foot or so below the top of the arched entrance.

There was no other way. The Death Merchant charged the

43

room, throwing himself forward, half-rolling and hitting the floor with his shoulder just inside the entrance, right next to where Vera Istenova was lying. He rolled sideways, away from her, as his eyes made an instant survey of the place. He saw them, the two of them, crouched on either side of the archway, flattened against the white-washed wall: an Arab dressed in burnoose and kaffyeh, looking in shock and surprise at Camellion and holding in one hand a 9 MM Walther pistol; and another man in dark slacks and gaudily colored sports shirt, his hands full of a Russian-made machine pistol.

Cursing in Russian, the GRU expert tried to bring his weapon to bear on Camellion. He almost succeeded, but his effort was an exercise in futility. He simply wasn't fast enough, nor good enough. Twice the Death Merchant pulled the trigger of the Magnum, and the Russian agent jumped as though hit by a freight train! A big hole opened up in his pretty sports shirt, directly in the center of his chest, and his head fell awkwardly to one side while his jugular vein, severed by the second .365 slug, began spurting a fountain of thick red, each spurt weakening with his dwindling heart beat.

The Commie joker was dead before he got halfway to the floor. Even so, the reflex of death tightened his trigger finger and the machine pistol came to life, sending a vicious stream of slugs over Camellion's head, across the room into a packing case standing against the wall. One slug must have hit a nailhead, as it ricocheted and grazed Camellion's left ankle, making him jerk and gasp in pain.

Automatically—one of his feet touching the corpse of Vera Istenova—the Death Merchant flattened himself to the dirty stone floor, firing at the Son of Allah by sheer instinct.

Frantically, the Arab sent a wild shot at Camellion, the slug cutting a tiny ditch across Camellion's back—a white hot streak of agony that interfered with Richard's own aim. Not that it really mattered! Instead of Camellion's slug entering the Arab's chest, it plowed into his mouth, moving upward at an angle, and blew the top of his head off.

Camellion thought of Hot Springs, Arkansas as he watched the river of red running from the Arab's mouth. The corpse dropped the Walther and slid slowly downward. The dead man finally arrived at his destination, sitting down flat on the floor, leaning stupidly against the wall, his eyes wide open and blood staining his pointed beard . . .

Slipping slightly on the floor, Richard got quickly to his

feet and rushed over beside the packing case, motioning for Israela, who was rushing into the room, to move over beside him. She had taken off her gray-white wig and her long dark hair was falling over her neck and shoulders. The shopping bag was tied around her slim waist.

"You should have stayed in front!" Camellion snarled. "But now that you're here, keep down. The rest of them are probbably in the next room, or does that door lead to the outside?" He indicated a solid-looking door a few feet to one side of the packing case.

Israela shook her head. "The shop's much longer than this wall we're standing by," she whispered back. "That door has to lead to another room."

"Give me the UZI," Camellion said, "and a couple of smoke grenades."

He finished reloading the twin magnums.

"Wait for our men!" she said fiercely, putting a restraining hand on his shoulder. "You don't know how many of them are in there!"

"Do as I tell you!"

Giving him an odd look, as if to ask him why he wanted to do what amounted to sheer suicide, the girl slammed a fresh clip into the machine gun and handed the weapon to him; then, dipping into the shopping bag, she pulled out a couple of smoke canisters and handed them to him. In turn, he handed her the fully loaded Magnums, saying, "Stay here and cover the doorway, and wait for our side to arrive—and don't follow me! You're too young to die."

"You should wait!" Israela insisted angrily. "We want as many alive as we can get! Isser won't like this, your turning the place into a slaughter-house!"

"We have an agent for questioning!" Camellion ground out. "The man out in front—remember!" Thinking of Boris Sokolovskii and the Texas disguise the Russian agent had so cleverly used, he added, "As we say in Texas, you have to travel with the grass, which means we have to hit them hard —and now. Once those Commie goofs realize the show's completely off the road, they might even try to blow up the building. Isser wouldn't like that either. Now keep to the wall!"

Moving to one side of the door, Camellion slowly tried the handle—locked! A short burst of UZI slugs instantly unlocked the door and, still standing to one side, Camellion pulled it open.

45

A wild burst of machine gun fire greeted him, the hail of death speeding harmlessly past through the open doorway. While Israela stared at Camellion as though he were a madman, he yelled, "GIVE IT UP! WE'VE GOT THE BUILDING SURROUNDED!"

"Eedee Kchawrtoo!" a voice yelled back and another burst of slugs flashed by the Death Merchant. Then a voice in English, "Go to hell, you bastard!"

"But you'll go to the devil first!" Camellion said to himself. He pulled the pins of the smoke grenades, tossed them into the room, counted to three, then rushed through the open door, crouching low and spraying the room with machine gun fire. He knew he would have only a minute or so, because he was no more immune to smoke than the Russian intelligence agents.

Vision was almost impossible through the rolling clouds of white smoke, but he saw one Russian—the son of a bitch looked like Khruschev!—leveling down on him with a Red Army Zortov pistol. The Commie didn't know it, but it was the last desperate act of his life. Between a fit of coughing, he did manage to get off a shot, and for a moment he thought he had succeeded in hitting the *grahzny* Jew! He was wrong. The slug had only grazed the Death Merchant's side, the sudden pain causing him to cry out and jerk to one side. But it was a movement of agony that saved his life, that spoiled the aim of the Ivan with the machine gun. A line of slugs passed within six inches of Camellion, burying themselves in the wall, but not before scattering a large plaster statue of St. Ann.

Coughing now, his eyes burning from the smoke, Camellion swivelled the UZI, moving the muzzle back and forth like one would use a garden hose. The Commie with the machine gun literally exploded as a couple of dozen slugs blew him apart. The other Ivan with the Zortov, the one who resembled Khruschev, didn't fare any better. He did try to get off another shot, but died even as his finger was pulling the trigger, a half dozen UZI slugs ripping into his upper chest and face. His heart gave a final beat, his face vanished and he died without uttering a single sound.

Yet even through the sound of gunfire, the Death Merchant could hear it. That familiar sound . . . the rapid clicking of a Vibroplex code key! He had to give the Russian agents credit. Even in the midst of dying they were still contacting Cairo— or was it The Center in the Soviet Union?—and apprising their superiors of the situation. Uh huh! The light will burn late in the Kremlin tonight!

Still another all too familiar sound! A loud ticking, similar to an alarm clock, that could mean only one thing: the Communist fanatics had the place boobytrapped. How long before the big bang?

Through the rolling clouds of smoke, the Death Merchant could barely see the man who was frantically working the telegraph key, sitting across the room in front of a short-wave set. Camellion moved quickly—and from the far side of the room a Zortov boomed. Another molten flash of pain ripped Camellion's left side, up high, a few inches below the arm pit, a tiny bit of hell which still didn't prevent him from sending a burst of UZI slugs in the direction from which the shot had come. There was a short scream and as Camellion bounded across the room he saw that the Russian had apparently been crouching to one side of the radio table, waiting for an opportunity to get Camellion in his sights. He wasn't trying any longer. He was only moaning, "Maxim, *puhmuhgeeteh mneh!*"

Fine—only Maxim, who was apparently the agent working the code key, couldn't even help himself. He glanced up, his finger still tapping the sending key, saw the Death Merchant almost on top of him, and tried to bring up his own machine pistol. Then his smoky world exploded in pain and darkness as Camellion slammed him across the head with the barrel of the UZI.

"You, we take alive, stupid," Camellion mumbled. Coughing incessantly, his eyes burning so intensely that he could hardly see, the Death Merchant began a hurried search for the source of the loud ticking: the timing-detonator that was connected to—what kind of explosives and how much?

In short order, he found the detonator to one side of the short wave set—a KBX type with an hour's running time! Holding the timer closer to his face, he stared at the dial. Only a few minutes' time! He knew he had no choice. His only chance now was to pull the wires! You couldn't reverse the time-knob with a KBX. And if the timer had a feed-back circuit? He'd never know it! The moment he pulled the wires the feed-back would automatically detonate the explosives.

Now I lay me down to die, maybe!—and he jerked the two wires from the timing device. There was no explosion. The clicking stopped.

Camellion began tracing the wires which had been connected to the timer. They curled across the table and over the edge, down to a two-foot square box on the floor, to what must have been fifty or sixty pounds of plastic explosive! More than enough to blow up half the block! And it almost had.

The Death Merchant began staggering from the room, dragging the gut-shot agent, who was still moaning and the radio operator after him, almost collapsing in the arms of Jock Heydecker and three Israeli policemen who were rushing through the doorway.

Israeli police filled the Catholic Shop, in the front part of which Isser Lev Langbein was waiting with Israela Diamant. They stared at him, at his bullet-ripped clothes, where slugs had grazed his back, his leg and his side . . . at his bloodshot eyes burning and watering from the smoke.

"Thank God you're all right," Langbein said, "but damn it! Why didn't you wait for us? I wanted to take them alive, if possible. Here, you'd better sit down."

He motioned for one of the policeman to bring a chair from behind the counter. Camellion shook his head and eased himself up on the other counter, sitting down with his feet dangling a few inches above the floor. "It wasn't possible," he said calmly, "but we've got the radio operator and the agent who was acting as clerk. Israela, my Magnums."

Silently she handed him the big revolvers and he slipped them into his shoulder holsters. His eyes hurt and he wished he had a glass of cold tomato juice.

"But if you hadn't rushed the situation, we might have captured more!" the Chief of the Israeli Intelligence Service insisted.

Jock, who had joined them, clapped Camellion on the back. "Well, Isser, it's a jolly good thing our matey here did attack when he did," he said loudly. "There was enough fusil-plastic explosive back there to make half of Jerusalem go boom. And only a minute and a half to go when laddie boy here pulled the wires! The ruddy GRU chaps 'ave a 'abit of blowing themselves up when cornered!"

Israela said, "We'll have three Russians to question if the third one doesn't die." She turned to Langbein. "I'm curious as to how all these Russian agents could operate in Jerusalem. I'll bet they're 'illegals' who slipped in as European Jews."

Langbein sighed. "We'll know after we investigate," he said. Jock looked around the shop, amazement in his gray eyes.

48

"By God! It was a bloody good show. Those ruddy bastards sure put up a good fight!"

The four of them watched as two Israeli policemen carried out on a stretcher the corpse of Vera Istenova, one of whose hands was dragging along the floor . . . moving at times as if waving goodbye. Camellion's hand came up in a smart salute!

"Pruhshcheye teh!" he said, telling her goodbye in Russian. "Too bad you had to be on the wrong side . . ." Then he said to Israela, his eyes searching her face, "You did a fine job. You react well in an emergency."

"You didn't think I would, did you?" Smoking a cigarette, she regarded him with puzzled eyes. She tilted her chin, but there was no resentment in her words.

"I never lie, never cheat and never apologize," Richard replied, swinging his legs back and forth. He paused for a moment and his voice became tender. "But in your case I'll make an exception. I was wrong about you. I'm sorry."

Concealing her surprise, Israela smiled. She felt that Richard Camellion had a lot in common with a drunk! An alcoholic was either slobbering in the gutter or praying under a halo! Camellion also seemed to go from one extreme to the other. He was either an angel or a devil . . . either cold-blooded or soft-hearted. And because she knew that one's real life was seldom the life one led, she wondered what Richard Camellion was actually like.

Or, as his nickname implied, did he truly enjoy violence and death?

Israel felt that the coming weeks would reveal the answer . . .

CHAPTER V

Proud that he, a man of sixty-four winters, had "second sight" and didn't have to wear glasses, Doctor Yuri Popvikin, acknowledged as the best bio-parapsychologist in the Soviet Union, stretched out his long legs, sank deeper in the wicker chair and looked at the schedule which Colonel Kagorin had just handed him. Sniffing, he dabbed at his nose with a pale green handkerchief. This dry Egyptian climate! Not at all agreeable to his sinuses.

Reading the schedule, Popvikin nodded mechanically, his watery eyes blinking rapidly—those idiots in the Kremlin! He moved his almost bone-like fingers through his sparse gray hair while anger rose within him. Positively not! Those ignorant savages were attempting to rush the process! Why couldn't the Kremlin and those MVD clods realize that the creative process could not be forced? A scientist was not a slave, except to science! Imagine! Putting a "schedule" on perfecting a device as scientifically important as the Psychotron! Those political fools and their silly dreams of conquest!

"This will not do, Colonel!" Dr. Popvikin said in disgust. "This will not do at all." He handed the paper back to Kagorin, glaring at him and at Victor Gulyaiev who was also in the AMTORG office, sitting beside Kagorin's desk. "My Psychotron will not be ready for the supreme test for telepathic hypnosis for a least a month. Dr. Sergeyev and I are still taking the bugs out of the Alpha Wave Sensor, which is a kind of Pavlovian conditioner. I shall explain. Alpha waves are one of four brain wave frequencies. Typical frequencies of Alpha rhythms are between eight and ten Hz or cycles per second. Other frequencies may be higher or lower than this and are called Beta, Theta and Delta. My Psychotron controls all four frequencies. What we do is to channel the—"

"I am not interested in the technical aspects of your mind wrecker!" Alexis Kagorin almost shouted, close to shaking in anger. But with a gigantic effort of will, he managed to control himself and continued in a more normal tone. "We have a schedule to maintain, Doctor, and Moscow expects us to maintain that schedule!"

Popvikin snorted in annoyance! "Huh! What do those narrow-minded idiots in Moscow know?" he piped in a high voice. "I ask you, Colonel! What do they know about science? You can tell those peanut minds in the Kremlin that in the laboratory we don't work with our eyes on a time clock and our minds fastened to a stupid schedule; and you can put what I have just said into your ridiculous report, as I'm more than sure you will!"

Watching the two men, the freckled-faced GRU chief and the fragile-looking Doctor Popvikin who resembled Leon Trotsky, Victor Gulyaiev was absolutely certain that Colonel Kagorin would do just that: by diplomatic courier, he would faithfully dispatch the recording of the meeting to The Center for evaluation.

Victor mulled over what Popvikin had just said . . . words bordering on treason, opinions that would have sent other men to the labor camps for life. Yet Victor knew that nothing would happen to the brilliant bio-parapsychologist. Popvikin was too valuable a scientist, too indispensable to the Kremlin's plans for world domination, so important a man that the GRU Apparat in Cairo had strict orders to cater to his every whim and to give him anything within reason he wanted, as long as his desires did not interfere with his work on the Psychotron or endanger the security of the espionage cell. Sensibly, Moscow treated him like a spoiled child, even keeping him supplied with *Kvahs,* a drink made by the simultaneous acid and alcoholic fermentation of rye, wheat, barley, or buckwheat meal; and with *Kisehl,* a kind of sourish jelly made of lindenberries.

Victor Gulyaiev respected Dr. Popvikin, unlike Kagorin who believed that scientists were idealistic fools unable to comprehend or to cope with reality—"big brained boobs" to whom the subtleties of power and force were strangers.

"The muzzle of a gun is far more effective than a test tube!" Kagorin was fond of saying; nevertheless, he still followed—and very faithfully, too—The Center's orders to handle Popvikin with gloves that were extra soft and fluffy, and he never apprised Popvikin of any complications that might make operations difficult—like last night's catastrophe!

Victor felt nauseous every time he thought of how the

Catholic Shop had been shot to pieces by that damned Death Merchant! Impossible! But it had happened!

He and Kagorin had been glued to the short wave set, listening to the vital 10:30 report from the *Mokryye Dela* Apparat in Jerusalem. Maxim Bashkirs had been at the code key, his expert touch more than recognizable to both Victor and Alexis. Expectantly they had listened as he tapped out the bad news: Neither Nikhail Tuvalov nor Boris Sokolovskii had been seen at the Catholic Shop; nor had Anwar, their Syrian *fedayeen* driver, put in an appearance.

Bashkirs requested information and instructions: 1) What had gone wrong? Did "Polar Bear"—the code name for the Cairo Apparat—know what had happened? 2) Request orders and instructions: Top Priority action schedule, please:

A long pause! And then it happened! Kagorin and his chief assistant sat there, stunned as the dots and dashes told them that the Catholic Shop was being attacked!

IT MUST BE THE WORK OF THE ISRAELI SECURITY POLICE! Maxim frantically tapped out. A MAN AND WOMAN DISGUISED AS AN OLD COUPLE ARE SHOOTING IT OUT WITH SOME OF THE OTHERS IN THE FRONT OF THE SHOP. WE WILL ATTEMPT TO TRAP THEM IN THE MIDDLE ROOM. IF THEY GET THIS FAR WE WILL KILL THEM AND AS MANY OF THE POLICE AS WE CAN AND BLOW UP THE SHOP. I THINK THE OLD MAN IS NOW IN THE MIDDLE ROOM. I—

Another long pause. HE'S IN THE BACK ROOM AND FIGHTING IT OUT WITH THE OTHERS. I AM SETTING THE TIMER DETONATOR. I—LONG LIVE THE SOVIET UNIO—

Silence! Victor and Alexis had stared at each other, both knowing who the "old man" had been! Only Richard Camellion, the Death Merchant, moved with such terrible speed and deadly efficiency! Only the Death Merchant could wipe out an entire espionage unit—and a *Mokryye Dela* one at that! And that's what worried Alexis Kagorin: were they all dead, or had some members of the unit survived, to be carried off by the Shin-Bet and questioned? Even so, not a single member of the Jerusalem Apparat knew the location of the Psychotron complex; not a single one knew the details regarding the extreme security measures with which Dr. Popvikin and his staff were guarded. Another possibility was that the Catholic Shop had been blown off the face of the earth. If so, was the Death Merchant dead? But suppose the son of a bitch wasn't? Suppose he had managed to get out before the detonator touched off the explosives?

Thinking of last night's debacle, Victor Gulyaiev concluded that Death was always a quicker thing than a funeral —and a lot less melancholy. Victor smiled slightly as he heard Popvikin screeching in his treble-screaky voice. "Colonel, you had better make it clear to those cabbageheads in Moscow that I will not tolerate their ridiculous and impossible demands! I'm a scientist and a Russian and I love my country, but I'm not a brain-washed bumpkin who believes all those stupid Communist slogans! Don't sit there, Colonel, and tell me we must work with greater speed for the 'glory of the Party!' Your doing that makes you look like an ass!"

Angrily, Popvikin reached into the top pocket of his coat and pulled out a smelly old pipe. He began methodically stuffing it with tobacco which he patiently tapped from a tin that had been in his left hip pocket.

Victor Gulyaiev's sneaky gaze travelled from Popvikin's face—the scientist always looked as if he were smelling something rancid!—to Kagorin's freckled features, now purple with rage! He wondered if Alexis would be able to control himself; he also wondered if Popvikin could hear the soft hum of the tape recorder in Kagorin's desk. The Death Merchant! What would Kagorin do about him? Somehow Victor could not believe that Richard Camellion was dead. If the Catholic Shop had been blown up, why hadn't they heard about it over the Tel-Aviv Radio?

Breathing heavily in frustration, Colonel Kagorin stared maliciously at the scientist, wishing he could put his hands around Popvikin's chicken-like neck and squeeze and squeeze and squeeze!

Filthy words of treason! That's what the senile old idiot had uttered. But the catch was that the stinking old shit was a very important scientist of the Union of Soviet Socialist Republics—probably the most important in the entire world, considering the tremendous potential of the Psychotron! Still, he had spoken treason! Damn it! Not only had he poked fun at the Communist Party, but at the Leaders! Within a few days The Center would be listening to his every word, to every word that had been spoken at the meeting. "Humor"

53

Popvikin, the directive ordered. Keep him "happy" and "contented."

The well-oiled wheels of self-preservation turned swiftly in Kagorin's mind, calculating . . . weighing the odds. If he didn't at least berate Popvikin for his vicious and slanderous attack against the government, what would General Semichastny, the Director General of the GRU *Otdel* think? Semichastny might even think he agreed with Popvikin. Better to play it safe!

Kagorin's pig-shaped eyes glowed fiendishly as he watched Dr. Popvikin puffing out thick clouds of smoke. "Doctor," he said, his voice as sharp as a cracking of a bull whip, "I cannot, under any conditions, permit you to besmirch and malign our glorious nation and its wise leaders. Your brazen aspersions against the Party are as vile and vindictive as the lying accusations of the Western imperialist nations, such as the United States that—"

"Oh shut up, Colonel," Popvikin said mildly, "you sound like a paragraph out of Pravda!" He continued to puff contentedly on his pipe, hoping he might have irked Kagorin to the breaking point! A display of temper by Kagorin would be just the thing for the tape recorder going in the desk— *the one the idiot thinks I don't know about! That Communist Party lackey! If there's anything I despise worse than a man who derives pleasure from making others feel uncomfortable, it's a man who'd sell his own mother's soul for his own ends, for his own security—and Kagorin has both faults!*

Closing his hands into tight fists, Kagorin put them on his desk. He glared balefully at the scientist. He'd fix the big brained boob! "Thank you, Doctor," he said smugly. "Coming from a deviationist like yourself, I consider your words about Pravada a high compliment and I'm sure Moscow will remember what you've said."

Also thinking of the tape recorder in the desk and of how the conversation would be analyzed at GRU headquarters, Victor Gulyaiev said forcefully, "You shouldn't be so juvenile, Doctor. Our government gives you the best equipment in the world to work with, yet all you do is complain! You should be ashamed of yourself!"

Kagorin grinned crookedly, running his tongue over his lower lip. "Of course he's ungrateful, Victor. He has complete freedom in his work, but still he's not appreciative!"

Freedom! The word was like stale vomit in Popvikin's

mouth! The very sound of the word almost gagged him, and well it should! Under Stalin, he had spent three years in a labor camp near Vilyuisk. Andrew, his younger brother had been arrested, charged with "political deviation" and shot!

Freedom! The Communist Party swine didn't even know the meaning of the word!

Wisely, Dr. Popvikin refrained from voicing his bitter thoughts and remembrances, knowing that he had already said enough, that he had gone as far as he dared. No sense in angering the men in the Kremlin beyond the point of no return, to the extent that their resentment would force them to clap him in an insane asylum! That was the latest method for silencing political dissidents: to have them certified "psychotic" and dragged off to some mental hospital!

Stalin had once said, *Zhit stalo legche, zhit stalo veselei!* —Life has become easier, life has become more cheerful! Well, life wasn't easier, and it certainly wasn't more cheerful!

Popvikin was no fool, more than realizing there wasn't anything he could do to change the system. He was a scientist, not a political revolutionary; yet because his basic sense of justice rebelled at such hypocrisy, he took one last final dig at the espionage chief. "I didn't come here to listen to propaganda, Kagorin," he said. "You people have taken me from my work, have forced me to lose an entire day, but still insist that I speed up the test schedule on the Psychotron! You could have told me the same nonsense by messenger!"

"I had my reasons for sending for you, Doctor," Kagorin said, glancing at the tall window through which the bright mid-afternoon sun was streaming, making a weird, hot pattern on his desk. Pushing back his swivel chair, Alexis got up, strode over to the window and pulled the drapes. He returned to his desk, sat down, and once more turned his attention to Dr. Popvikin, who was sniffing loudly and dabbing at his nose with a handkerchief.

"I sent for you, Doctor, because I wanted you to report in person," Kagorin said. "And as you very well know, security does not permit our committing such valuable matters to paper."

"And I've given you my report," Dr. Popvikin said icily. "I have told you that it will be at least a month—maybe less, maybe longer—before my device is ready for the testing of its capability to induce telepathic hypnosis. And even Brezhnev, Kosygin and Podgorny can't change that fact!

Damn it, don't you people realize you can't put a time limit on the kind of research we're doing! You know, we're not digging ditches out there in the desert!"

Popvikin tapped the bowl of his pipe against his open palm, knocking ash from it. Getting up from the wicker chair, he dropped the ashes into a spotlessly clean silver ashtray on Kagorin's desk, not missing the pained look in Kagorin's eyes as he did so.

"I also wanted to inform you in person that we've canceled the Jerusalem test," Alexis Kagorin continued in a more friendly voice. He felt that he had properly chastised Popvikin for his slanderous attack against the Government and that The Center would be satisfied. Why continue to antagonize the cantankerous old son of a bitch! Half-smiling, he said pleasantly, "So you see, Doctor, you and your staff no longer have to divide your efforts between the main experiment and the portable Psychotron unit."

Dr. Popvikin sniffed loudly, like a snotty-nosed six-year-old. "Why the cancellation?" he asked curiously. "Only a few weeks ago you were pressing us for the completion of JER-C-1, and now that we're on the brink of success, you say to forget it and devote full time to the main unit!"

"The answer is very simple. Moscow felt that a cancellation of JER-C-1 would permit you and your staff to devote full time toward the completion of the device for the main telepathic test. That is why the schedule has been set up. Isn't that obvious to you?"

Victor Gulyaiev reinforced his boss' lie. "How can you say that you can't devote full time to the main Psychotron, now that you no longer have to concern yourself with the portable unit? What are you people doing out there in the desert—drinking vodka and playing chess?"

"I can't commit myself!" Popvikin screeched, half rising from his chair. "There are too many variables! You fools think you can kill time without injuring eternity! How can I tell you unequivocally that by such and such a time the Psychotron will be completed? I can't! You're asking the impossible!"

"That seems like a poor excuse to me!" Victor snapped. Even as he spoke, he wondered what Popvikin's reaction would be if he knew the real reason for the cancellation of JER-C-1: because the Death Merchant had shot the living hell out of the Jerusalem espionage cell.

"What about C-A-18?" Popvikin asked.

"Bir El Tamadeh is still scheduled for the same date—July 15th," Kagorin said quickly, leaning back in his chair. "I'll fly to the desert base for the experiment. I'd like to learn more about your marvelous Psychotron. I know so little about the weapon."

For that matter, Alexis Kagorin knew little about Dr. Yuri Popvikin—only the essentials contained in the political file of the scientist. No doubt about it, Popvikin was a brilliant man, and Moscow considered him a genius. At one time, he had been professor of biology at Moscow University. Then, with Doctor Vasili Sergeyev, a physicist, he had established the scientific principle that all living matter, from a seed to a human being, is surrounded by electro-dynamic fields. A year later the two men had invented a device that could detect and measure magnetic and electrostatic "biological" fields. Four years later came the Psychotron, but while the device could cause permanent insanity and even death, by scrambling the four frequencies of the brain, its range was short. There was also another obvious drawback: the weapon only accomplished what conventional weapons could do—KILL! Plus the fact that killing with the Psychotron also was more complicated. However, the device had other possibilities! Telepathic hypnosis at long range! Ahh, that was something else! To be able to control an entire enemy population without destroying their cities—that was the ultimate weapon! The nation that had such a weapon could very easily rule the world!

Dr. Yuri Popvikin said stiffly, "I should be happy to explain the operation of the Psychotron to you during the next test, Colonel, but now I'd like to get back to work, unless there are other matters you feel we should discuss."

Alexis Kagorin pressed a button on his desk, and a moment later six security agents grimly entered the room—Dr. Popvikin's escort to the heliport, to the copter that would fly him back to the hidden Psychotron base near the city of Suez.

After Popvikin and his escort had left the room, Victor got up and, going over to the long couch, sprawled out on it, putting his hands underneath his head and crossing his legs, his two feet resting on the far arm. He watched Kagorin open the desk drawer and switch off the tape recorder . . .

57

listened as the GRU colonel growled, "You know, Victor, one of these days Moscow's going to get fed up with that old fool's insults. Mark my words, Victor—Popvikin's asking for it!"

He pulled a watch from his pocket and checked its time against that of the grandfather clock standing against the far wall. Not bad. Only one second off.

"I was thinking about Assad," Victor said. "Why don't we have 'Evers' kill him? Our fat Egyptian friend, the Minister of the Interior, has never met Merkulov!"

"Yes, we could," mused Kagorin. "Merkulov will arrive from Paris tomorrow."

Continued Victor Gulyaiev, "It would be very simple for Merkulov to give him a dose of prussic acid via the 'tube.' Assad's known to have a heart condition, and since the gas leaves no trace, everyone would think he had a fatal attack of angina."

Kagorin turned in his chair so that he faced Victor. "The Center doesn't want us to kill Assad unless we have to. Anyhow, he isn't snooping any more than usual."

Victor thought for a moment. "It depends on how you want to evaluate what the fool might be thinking or what he eventually might do. As I told you earlier, when I flew to the base to pick up Popvikin, our security people told me that Assad was out there again yesterday, asking all sorts of questions."

Alexis Kagorin's eyes narrowed evilly. "Such as?"

Victor chuckled. "His logic was very sensible. He wanted to know why we have over a hundred security agents protecting what's supposed to be nothing more than a meteorological station . . . why we even feel it's necessary to ring the place with tanks. Suppose he had found the underground Psychotron room?"

"What else did the bastard ask?"

"Our boys told him that ultra-strict security was necessary because the station is so close to the damned Jews on the Sinai. And on the surface, he seemed to accept that explanation. But what about the next time Assad comes around, or the time after that? Alexis, what are we going to do about him?"

"The real danger lies in Assad's associating the destruction of Bel Sida with what's going on at the base," Kagorin said in a grim voice, "and now with C-A-18 coming up, should

58

he connect Bir El Tamadeh with the base—if he should do that we could have serious trouble with him!"

"But couldn't our Ambassador apply pressure to the Egyptian main office?" Victor asked. "That would certainly stop Assad!"

"Would it?" Kagorin wasn't so sure. "These damned Egyptians are too independent!" he snarled. "They accept our arms and technical aid, and yet the lice treat us as equals! You'd think they were doing us a favor!"

"Then for now we do nothing about Assad?" Victor said, sensing that Kagorin was very edgy. Well, the GRU chief had good reason to be: he was responsible for the success of the Psychotron experiments.

"It's the Death Merchant that worries The Center—and me." Alexis said in a low voice. "He's the *glavni vrag*—the main enemy we have to cope with! That's why Center is sending four SMERSH boys instead of two in order to kill the son of a bitch! Those artists in assassination will cut the life out of him, but finding him in Israel won't be easy."

Kagorin sighed deeply and began rubbing his chin thoughtfully; then he said, "We've got to be realistic, Victor. Do I have to tell you what will happen to us if Camellion somehow manages to get to Popvikin and the Psychotron! You know as well as I how vindictive General Semichastny can be."

Startled at Colonel Kagorin's frankness, and surprised that his Chief should admit to being so worried, Victor sat up on the couch, fumbling in his shirt pocket for his cigarettes. "No, Alexis," he said. "Camellion isn't likely to even get close to the base. The Death Merchant might be a one man army, but let's be practical: he still is only one man!"

Giving Kagorin quick nervous glances, Victor lit his cigarette, his breath catching in his throat over Alexis' reply.

"It wouldn't surprise me if Camellion didn't try to attack this place!" Alexis said bitterly. "Amtorg headquarters is no secret, and the Shin-Bet know we're here!" Very suddenly he turned in his swivel chair and banged his fist on the desk. "I tell you, Victor, that damned Death Merchant is the cause of all our present trouble! I'll tell you something else: if he does manage to interfere with the Psychotron experiments, you and I will be finished!"

The grandfather clock across the room began chiming the hour, and Kagorin, hurriedly pulling the watch from his pocket, began checking its time.

An icy feeling of dread began shivering up Victor Gulyaiev's spine. He sat there smoking . . . thinking of how cold it got in Siberia . . . thinking of how terrible it would be if he had to spend the remainder of his life there . . .

CHAPTER VI

NEVER talk if captured by the enemy, no matter what they do to you—and kill yourself if you can. Basil Nevsky thought of this GRU directive, trying to keep it from torturing his consciousness. A graduate of the Soviet Military Academy and of the GRU's Higher School in Moscow, Basil sat in a straight-backed wooden chair in a small room, his wrists handcuffed to the arms, his head swathed in bandages, his face as inexpressive as the Rock of Gibraltar. How could he kill himself?

He sat brooding, his emotions a tornado of raging shame. To think that he had been taken so easily, like a rank amateur—he, who had been so thoroughly trained? There had been four years in internal security, intelligence and law at the Higher School's Juridical Institute, plus "American English" and Special Methods for Eliminating Enemies of the Soviet State. At twenty-four, Basil had been the youngest graduate of his class and had graduated with honors. All that hard studying and precious training—and then three years in the field: in London, Buenos Aires, Washington, D.C., and finally as an "illegal" in Jerusalem. Now—to find himself shackled like a common criminal and at the mercy of the enemy! It was degrading.

A round-faced young man with skin so smooth and shiny that it seemed to be drawn tight, like a drum skin, Basil thought about the—and that's what it was—a nightmare! The speed and suddenness with which it had happened! Nervous like the others in the Jerusalem Apparat because no one knew what had happened to the kidnap team and to the Death Merchant, Basil had been in the front of the Catholic Shop, functioning in his cover as "clerk," when the couple had walked in. They had been interested in purchasing one of their emotional opiates, one of their religious amulets, a statue of their Saint Joseph.

Basil recalled placing the statue on the counter. Then the sudden blurred glint of a gun barrel! Intense pain in the side of his head. Awakening the next morning in a hospital bed, handcuffed, with a headfull of headache! Had they pumped him full of pentothal or mendocaine? The slight tingle in his left arm and the acid taste in his mouth told him that they had. Ha—they couldn't have learned anything! His pre-conditioning with hypnotic feed-back had been instilled by experts.

The following day the Jew pigs had brought him to this place, to what he assumed was the Shin-Bet center in Jerusalem, and questioned him.

We know your real name is not Benjamin Kawaldawitz! they had said.

We know you're not a Polish Jew and that you're a GRU 'illegal!'

How did you manage to get into Israel?

We know you're a member of a special 'Blood Wet' unit —we learned that from Mikhail Tuvalov. What was the mission of your Apparat?

"Go to hell!" Basil had told them in perfect English, feeling smug at the time. Their questions indicated that he had not told them anything while under the influence of truth drugs. Let them question him all they wanted, even torture him, but he would not talk—NEVER!

However, the mention of Mikhail Tuvalov filled Basil with a sense of utter failure. So, Operation *Snegopa* had failed after all. The Death Merchant had not been captured.

In spite of his outward detachment, Basil Nevsky was afraid. An intelligent man, he did not want to die fearing the Unknown, although he had been an atheist since childhood. *But how could he possibly live?* he asked himself. The Israelis, knowing he was a Russian espionage agent, had every right to shoot him—and life imprisonment wouldn't be any better. Or, if he received a prison sentence, the Israelis might eventually exchange him for one of their own. *No!* Basil's logic quietly told him. He was not that important.

The cancer of uncertainty continued to increase his doubts and fears. What had happened to Gregory, who also had been clerking in the shop? To Vera Istenova? Had Lubinski, Nikolai, Maxim and the rest of them been killed or captured? No—NO—*NO! Impossible!* That could not have happened!

Inwardly a nervous wreck, Basil slyly watched the two men guarding him. One was obviously an Englishman, the short, wiry man whose name was "Jock." Odd it was, a Jew with an English accent! The other Moses moron, the tall, tubercular looking fellow, was probably a German Jew, judging from his accent. They called him "Ethan."

Jock Heydecker noticed the Russian watching him. "We'll be standing you up against a wall in a week or so, my boy," he said. "A pity too . . . all the girls and vodka you could have had. A pity that you'll be dying for a lost cause."

Basil remained silent, his lips clamped tightly together— one would have thought his mouth had been sewn shut! He was determined: he would never tell these Jew bastards what they wanted to know, not even his real name! And he'd commit suicide the first chance he got!

Try as he might, he could not keep his thoughts from returning to Kiev, where he had been born and had spent his early years. He thought of his parents, of his two brothers and three sisters. Most of all, he thought of Elana, his wife . . . sweet, dark-eyed Elana, whose voice was always laughter in his soul; and of Mark, his seven-month-old son. The knowledge that he would never see any of them again ate into his emotions, increasing his misery.

I might as well be dead, and in a week or so I guess I will be . . .

Catching him by surprise, the door opened, the suddenness of its inward swing snatching Basil from his deep pit of depression. Blank-faced, without showing the least trace of emotion, Basil evaluated the newcomers, trying to do so while staring straight ahead. He recognized all of them, except one, from the photographs given to the Apparat by The Center.

There—that man! He was the chief of the Shin-Bet! And the attractive young woman—Israela Diamant—damn her! The second man—Basil had never seen him before. He was an odd looking man, bald, except for a fringe of hair on the crown of his head, like the stupid monks of the old Orthodox Church, whose pictures Basil had seen in books. The man's front teeth protruded slightly, and his whole face was lit up in a smile, giving it a quality of warmth and cheer.

The third man! Only recently his photograph had been dispatched to the Jerusalem Apparat—a man who moved as though his muscles were coiled springs . . . who walked with an air of supreme confidence . . . whose hair was close-cut, but whose blue eyes burned with a strange fire—flame in pure ice!

Basil recognized him instantly: Richard Camellion, the

63

dreaded Death Merchant! The most dangerous man in the Middle East!

The GRU agent knew he was in for another round of questioning from the way the Shin-Bet people began placing chairs around him in a semi-circle.

"Well, Basil Nevsky, how do you feel this afternoon?" Isser Lev Langbein asked good-naturedly. Basil's eyes flickered in surprise. "Oh yes, my friend, we know who you really are," Langbein went on, "from papers found in the Catholic Shop. We even have the code book you use to contact 'Polar Bear.' I hope Colonel Kagorin doesn't hold you responsible."

"We also 'ave two of your Comrades," Jock Heydecker said. "Mikhail Tuvalov and Maxim Bashkirs. The rest of your unit is dead."

Ethan Friedenthal said in a low voice, "We even have it partially figured how all of you slipped into Israel—disguised as Jewish refugees from various parts of Europe. That's how you did it, wasn't it?"

Basil Nevsky remained as mute as the sphinx, and as impassive. God damn them! Everything they had said was the truth! He glared at the grim faces surrounding him, determined not to give them the least bit of cooperation.

"The only hitch was that your cell couldn't foresee that the agents who were supposed to kidnap me would fail in their efforts and that I'd manage to capture Mikhail Tuvalov for questioning," the Death Merchant said. He took a small box of raisins from his coat pocket and began tossing them into his mouth, one by one.

"And Tuvalov talked faster than an American used car salesman when under the influence of truth drugs," the man with the monk's fringe said. He was Simon Avidan, one of Langbein's advisers. "He talked and talked and talked . . ."

Langbein spoke up: "That's how we discovered your Apparat in the Holy City, from what Tuvalov told us. There's only one thing we need: for you to tell us what your mission was. You terror specialists were there for a specific reason. What was that reason?"

"You're also going to tell us the location of the Mind Blaster base in Egypt!" the Death Merchant surprised Basil by saying. "And one way or another, you *are* going to tell us."

Glaring at the ring of faces, Basil Nevsky sneered. "You're lying! You didn't obtain a single piece of information from

Tuvalov, anymore than you got anything out of me last night," he said. "Our psychological pre-conditioning is too thorough, and you know it!"

Israela, smoking a cigarette, laughed cheerfully and crossed her legs, turning slightly to Langbein, "This Ivan has a lot to learn, hasn't he?"

Slowly, Isser nodded his head and said in a tired voice, "Camellion, tell him why Tuvalov talked—and you're right, Nevsky! Under ordinary circumstances, Tuvalov wouldn't have mumbled a word."

The Death Merchant popped another raisin into his mouth. "Tuvalov talked because I'd smashed out all his front teeth," he said lazily. He glanced in Langbein's direction. "I suggest we let him see for himself."

Langbein nodded to Jock, who got up and left the room.

Fastening his cold eyes on the Russian agent, Camellion continued, "You can well imagine the pitiful condition Tuvalov was in by the time he received medical attention. Because he was extremely weak, the pentothal had what might be described as a 'double effect.' Tuvalov talked all right, and because he did, you're sitting there in that chair."

Reaching out, Camellion took hold of Basil's chin. "Hmmmm, you've got nice teeth too. I'll tell you something, my Russian friend. I wouldn't hesitate for a moment to pull all your teeth, if by so doing I could learn the location of the Mind Blaster complex. But I'm not concerned, you'll tell me before I'm finished with you."

Basil Nevsky smiled thinly. The world was full of little men, all of them living in a constant fear of death. Basil Nevsky did not intend to be one of them; yet his moon face paled when Jock appeared in the doorway with Mikhail Tuvalov, whose mouth was literally wired together! For many long seconds, Basil stared at the other Russian agent. By God! They had told the truth! The Death Merchant had smashed Tuvalov's upper jaw!

"Naturally he talked before we wired his jaw," Camellion explained to Basil. "We had a devil of a time understanding him . . ."

The chair on which Camellion was sitting spraddle-legged was reversed, its back facing him. He put his chin on the rounded top of the back, and his gaze knifed into Nevsky's face. "Where's the Psychotron base in Egypt?" Richard asked in a deadly voice.

65

"What was the mission of your Apparat in Jerusalem?" Langbein asked.

Simon Avidan moved his chair closer to the Russian agent. "Son, you might as well tell us what we want to know and save us all a lot of time. We've already gotten quite a bit from Bashkirs. Why don't you fill in the gaps?"

Avidan studied the Russian agent closely, but did not detect a flicker of emotion in the man's sweat-flecked face. Did Nevsky believe him, or did he suspect the real truth, which was that Bashkirs, too, had been immune to pentothal and had resisted conscious interrogation. All morning they had bombarded Bashkirs with questions, the answers to which he had firmly refused to give. Now, in another part of the building, other Shin-Bet agents were trying to wear him down.

Israela Diamant said, "You might as well cooperate, Nevsky. You're not going to get any sleep until you do. Tell us where the Psychotron base is."

From Friedenthal—"Tell us about your mission here in the Holy City."

Camellion again—"Where is the Psychotron base?"

Basil Nevsky turned on them like a mortally wounded animal caught in a trap. "Amateurs!" he hissed, leaning forward. "You're all a bunch of amateurs." His eyes darted from face to face. "Your threats don't impress me in the least," he spit out, "especially yours, Death Mercant. Break my teeth! Or my arms, or my legs. Put a bullet in my knees —but you won't learn a single thing from me. You're going to shoot me anyway, eventually. Why tell you anything?"

"Shoot you!" Israela exclaimed. "You have a morbid imagination! We don't go around bumping off people, not even *Mokryye Dela* spies, unless we have to!"

"But we'll make you wish you were dead!" Langbein said grimly.

Basil Nevsky merely stared at them. Again, for some odd reason, a vision of his wife burst in his mind—Elana, waving goodbye to him . . . standing there on the platform of the Kiev railroad station, holding little Mark in her arms. It occurred to Basil that was the sickness of modern times— people always waving goodbye, but nobody ever waving back.

In accordance with a pre-arranged plan, Camellion got up and pulled Nevsky in his chair to one side of the room, a portion of whose wall was pock-marked with bullet holes.

He then returned to his own chair, reversed it, and sat down in a normal manner, after which he pulled a Magnum from its holster. The others moved back, allowing him plenty of room.

Setting his jaw, Nevsky looked calmly at the Death Merchant, his expression one of resistance and perseverance.

"Basil, old buddy, where is the Psychotron base in Egypt?" Richard Camellion asked in the quiet tone that always brought the others to silence.

"In President Sadat's bedroom!" the Russian answered with a low laugh.

The Death Merchant triggered off two shots with such incredible speed that the explosions sounded almost as one! The Shin-Bet people stared at Nevsky, who now had a bloodly cut in the outer edge of each ear lobe, a small blood-filled nick as if touched by an extra-sharp straight razor!

Basil Nevsky didn't move. He continued to stare straight ahead of him, as though the people in the room didn't exist.

"The Psychotron base," Camellion said, thinking that the Russian had a lot of guts. "Where is the Psychotron base in Egypt?"

"What was your Apparat's mission in Jerusalem?" Langbein insisted.

Only silence from Basil Nevsky!

Again the Magnum flashed in the Death Merchant's hand —another wall-shaking roar! Instantly a blood line appeared on Nevsky's left cheek, where the steel-jacketed slug had skipped across it.

Basil Nevsky laughed, a low nervous laugh, even though he was trembling slightly.

"We heard you were one of the best marksmen in the world," he said with remarkable composure, "and you've proved it—only I know you're not about to shoot me! Moral swine like yourself never shoot unarmed men! That's one of your weaknesses. Even if you could kill me, you still wouldn't have any answers. As I said before, you're all amateurs."

Nevsky laughed again. "Care to try for the other cheek, Death Merchant?" he taunted.

Camellion cleared the Magnum of the used cartridges and pushed three fresh shells into the cylinder. Then he holstered the .357, stood up and buttoned his sports coat.

"Where are you going, Richard?" Israela asked, puzzled.

"I need a glass of cold tomato juice," he replied as he walked from the room.

For the remainder of the afternoon and all during the night they flung questions at Basil Nevsky—and got nowhere. They tried pentothal. Again—failure.

Toward dawn, it was Camellion who, evolving a scheme to make the Russian answer their questions, explained what he had in mind, concluding with, "Analysis of the oppressed mentality and the psychopathic personality that accrue from contact with the prevarications of GRU strategy must be carefully integrated with the analysis of the source. All men have one thing that is important to them, and so does Nevsky!"

Langbein said thoughtfully, "It might just work. We've tried everything else."

"So let's have a go at what Richard suggests," Israela said.

"Blimy!" Jock exclaimed. "I hope it does. Me eyes are so heavy they feel like they've been weighed with anvils!"

Israela agreed. "Huh!" she snorted, "that Russian's more awake than we are!"

Once more they confronted Basil Nevsky, who regarded them through red-rimmed eyes. He was prepared for the worst, had steeled himself for death and felt that he would die a hero. He might even be awarded a medal posthumously. Elana would be very proud of him . . .

"You men get some sleep; we'll take over," Langbein told the other four Shin-Bet agents who had been verbally hammering away at Nevsky. Without a word, they left the interrogation room.

Sinking to a chair, Langbein sighed. "Well, Nevsky, it seems you're too much for us. We've tried everything, and I must admit, you've beaten us." He motioned to Jock. "Remove his cuffs. No use keeping him handcuffed to the chair any longer."

Israela lit a cigarette and sat down next to Camellion, who was solemnly tapping his finger against the tip of his nose, his eyes never leaving Basil Nevsky as he watched Jock remove the Russian's manacles.

Jock put the handcuffs in his pocket, and Nevsky, rubbing his wrists, looked around him in triumph. "You can shoot me

68

any time," he said stiffly. "I am more than ready to die, but don't expect me to tell you anything."

"You're free to go, Nevsky," Langbein said simply. Nevsky's lips parted slightly in surprise. "And if you want to remain in Israel," Langbein went on, "I'll personally see to it that you can obtain a special work permit."

The glow of victory in Nevsky's eyes was replaced first by puzzlement, then by extreme caution. "I see," he snapped. "You intend to execute me on the streets by arranging an accident! So that is how you Jews play the game."

Chewing on a small, unlit cigar, Jock Heydecker laughed, turned and grinned at Camellion. "Why the bloke doesn't trust us!" He jerked his attention back to Nevsky. "Me boy, the Chief means it. You're free—and we 'aven't arranged any 'accident' for you. You actually are free, and like he said, you can even stay in Israel and work. Say—would you like to go to a Kibbutz?"

Nevsky stared around him in amazement, having the look of a rather proud pheasant who suddenly finds himself on a flat, open plain surrounded by hunters!

"There is, of course, one catch," Isser said matter of factly. "We intend to leak it to Colonel Kagorin that you've talked, that in exchange for freedom you told us all we wanted to know—and Kagorin will believe it!"

"And even if he has his doubts, he'll have to proceed as though he did," Israela carefully pointed out. "So will The Center. That's how the game is played."

Camellion yawned, wishing he had picked up another box of raisins from the vending machine out in the hall. "We don't have to kill you, Nevsky," he said. "The Center will do that for us—and if you have any relatives back home . . . too bad, old buddy."

Langbein jerked a thumb toward the open doorway. "You're free, Nevsky," he said. "Get lost. We'll know where you are in Isreal and eventually your bosses in Moscow will, too."

Basil Nevsky stood as if his feet were nailed to the floor. He saw her again! Elana! Waving goodbye to him once more! Then the same sweet girl . . . slaving in a work camp . . . cold . . . undernourished . . . starving! Basil saw his son, Mark—in a State school! His parents, his brothers and sisters . . . either dead or worse, existing as the living dead! *Oh my God!*

Basil blinked stupidly at Langbein, who got up, stuck his

head out the door and called for a couple of Shin-Bet agents. Basil had to admit they were right: Colonel Kagorin would have to believe that he had talked and defected to the West, and just to be on the safe side, The Center would proceed on that assumption and instantly dispatch a team of SMERSH assassination specialists to track him down. General Semi-chastny would also take out his revenge on Nevsky's entire family and, beyond question of any doubt, ship them off to one of the worst of the labor camps, probably one close to the Arctic Circle.

That has to be it! Nevsky told himself desperately. This was another ploy, another clever trick to make him talk! *Of course—why they're not about to turn me loose. Whoever heard of such a thing! They can't turn me loose! Yet I haven't talked! Suppose—deciding that I'm not going to tell them anything—suppose they mean it? Suppose they actually are going to set me free, as their way of getting even with me? We've gotten rid of enemy agents that way! Why shouldn't the Shin-Bet?*

Two Shin-Bet men walked into the room and Langbein told them to take Nevsky out of the building. "Take him where he wants to go," Isser said. "If he can't think of a place," Langbein said, "dump him off anywhere in Jerusalem."

They might mean it! If they do let me go—? Terrible thoughts and possibilities whirled in confusion within Nevsky. Once more he thought of Elana!

He felt the fingers of the Shin-Bet men tighten on his arms.

"Get him out of here," Langbein ordered. "Let his own Center execute him!"

"WAIT!" Basil croaked, his voice shaking, his face anxious. "If—if I do tell you what you want to know—what will happen to me?"

Langbein's voice was flat. "At least a thirty-year sentence, maybe life!"

"You're bluffing. You can't afford to let me go!"

The Shin-Bet chief shook a finger at the Russian agent. "Whether we let you go or not, we can still make Kagorin think you've talked, and if you have a family, you know what your *Otdel* boss will do to them."

Basil Nevsky told them all he knew.

For the remainder of that day and part of the next, the Shin-Bet questioned the GRU agent, never giving him a moment's rest, allowing him only time to eat and sleep for a few hours. Nevsky's replies were always the same, his answers never varying.

It was almost noon and once more—for the 100th time—Isser Langbein asked him, "Basil, once more, tell us about your Apparat's mission."

"I've told you over and over," Nevsky said wearily, "our mission was to use a portable Psychotron in this area." He seemed almost pathetic in his misery, in his eagerness to convince them that he was telling the truth. "Please don't ask me how this portable unit was to be smuggled into Jerusalem or how it was supposed to work. I don't know. *I don't know!*"

"The Psychotron complex in Egypt—where is it located—*where?*" the Death Merchant lashed out savagely.

With pseudo-disgust, he pushed back his chair and stood up, directing his pretended disbelief at Langbein. "Isser, all he's telling us are lies and more lies. Acceptance of enslavement is deeply buried in pathogenic types such as he; it's the result of the sense of dread and anxiety which is the lot of all men under Communist rule. I'd throw him out if I were you."

Going along with Camellion's strategy, Isser pretended to agree. "Hmmmm, perhaps you're right. Maybe it might be a good idea to have him flown to Tel-Aviv and dropped off at Zina Square." Craftily his eyes stole back to Nevsky, who, inwardly, was almost in a panic.

"But I'm telling you the truth!" Basil shouted. "I don't know where the Psychotron base is! I've told you that a couple of hundred times! Only Kagorin, his top aides, and the Egyptian Minister of the Interior know! Honest! That's the truth!"

"There you go again, referring to Hasan El Assad!" the Death Merchant sneered. "You're lying, Basil. Worse, you're a fool if you think you can make us believe that a clever man like Kagorin would permit Assad knowledge of such a valuable secret—nor would The Center permit it!"

Nevsky held out his arms pleadingly and said quickly, the words tumbling from his mouth, "But I keep telling you, Assad doesn't realize he knows the location! In fact, his nosiness and the reality that he thinks the Psychotron complex is a meteorological station is a kind of joke in the Cairo Apparat!"

"Lies, all lies," smirked Israela. "You'll have to do better than that, Basil!"

"Damn it! I'm telling you the truth! Why won't you believe me?"

"How do you know that Assad is considered a joke?" Camellion snarled. He noticed that the Russian had amazingly long, thin fingers and that he was almost incapable of speaking, of expressing himself, without gesturing with them.

"Yes, tell us again how you know," Simon Avidan urged.

"Mikhail Tuvalov told us," Basil said slowly, "He was in Cairo only a month ago and was present when Colonel Kagorin and other agents were laughing about Assad! According to Mikhail, Assad's like a busybody of an old woman, always snooping around the complex asking questions. But he still doesn't know that the place is being used for the Psychotron experiments. He thinks it's only Meteorological Station 4-FD."

"And yet none of you know exactly where the complex is?" Camellion thrust his face very close to Basil's and grabbed the startled man by his shirtfront. "Tell me the truth! Answer me!"

"I swear I don't know!" the Russian replied in a choked voice, trembling, for staring into Camellion's eyes was like feeling the poetry of Death itself. "None of us in the Jerusalem Apparat knew. Just Kagorin and his special assistants and Assad—only Assad has no idea that he knows. I swear it!"

From Jock: "Why did Kagorin tell Assad about the base at all? That's what I find difficult to believe. Me boy, I think you're lying all over the place."

Basil replied instantly. "I've told you that. I've told you that we in the Apparat wondered that too. Mikhail said that Kagorin had to tell Assad. As Minister of the Interior, if Assad discovered an unreported base, his suspicions would instantly be aroused. This way, by knowing the meteorological station is there, he doesn't suspect what the base is really being used for."

Basil Nevsky gaped at the Shin-Bet people, his fearful eyes going from face to face. They stared back at him.

Later, when the Death Merchant and the others discussed what they had learned from the Russian agent, Langbein remarked that they were still check-mated.

"I believe that Russian," he said vigorously, "but we can't escape the fact that Assad's in Egypt. He might as well be on the planet Mars!"

Simon Avidan remarked with a half-laugh, "One of us might hop over to Cairo and ask Assad to give us the location of Meteorological Station 4-FD."

"Yeah . . . I know the blighter would bust a gut telling us!" Jock growled.

"That's exactly what I intend to do!" the Death Merchant said, "go to Egypt, kidnap Assad and force him to tell me where the station is!"

Five pairs of eyes turned to Camellion in amazement. "You can't—you're not really serious!" Langbein asked. "Such a wild scheme couldn't possibly succeed. Why, even you couldn't bring it off, Camellion!"

Israela smiled softly to herself. She knew the Death Merchant meant what he said. He was that kind of man—to grab the impossible and twist it into reality!

"Richard, I'm going with you," she said.

Camellion's eyes locked with hers. "Until now I thought you had good sense," he said. "But I won't take you. Going to Cairo is too dangerous."

He glanced over at Langbein, his gaze informing the Shin-Bet chief that he wanted him to tell Israela that she could not go along on the mission.

Langbein surprised the Death Merchant. "Taking her with you might be a good idea," he said. "You and she can go in as tourists, as a married couple . . ."

"You're not going," Camellion said to Israela.

Calmly she looked at him, then said, "It is better to dwell in the corner of the housetop than with a brawling woman and in a wide house! I am going with you."

The Death Merchant's mouth formed a trace of a smile. "Very well, I'd rather take you with me than have you quoting Proverbs to me."

Camellion felt strangely awake and ultra alive, as if all previous living had been a long, monotonous dream . . . as if his life were about to end.

He wondered how long he would continue to explore the astonishment of living!

CHAPTER VII

Because man is only miserable so far as he thinks himself so (as is written in the Koran), the Bedouins of the Sinai Peninsula, which is separated from Egypt by the isthmus of Suez, do not realize they are living in one of the most desolate regions of the world . . . an immense area of rock, sand, heat and emptiness that is nothing more than an irregular plateau, rising in the south to heights of over 8,000 feet. Over vast periods of time, erosion has given the uplands a scarred face, a countryside that almost resembles the surface of the moon . . . and over it all, a quietness and a loneliness, a stillness marred only by the whispering of the wind and the Jinns devils. Rainfall is scarce—about six inches per year along the northern coast, but only a scant two or three inches in the south. This, in conjunction with the great gorges, ravines and general inaccessibility of the mountainous regions, explains why the sparse population is to be found almost entirely in the northern half, for the northerly debouching wadies are broad and pockets of cultivation surround wells, such as Al 'Arish, Al Awja, El Nakhl and Bir El Tamadeh.

By modern standards, life in the Sinai is not very pleasant; nonetheless, it is still home to some *Badawi*, that "desert dweller" know to Westerners as Bedouin—those nomadic tribesmen who live in black goats' hair tents and subsist on products of animal husbandry . . . a livelihood determined by the grazing needs of their herds or flocks. And so it is that during the rainy winter season, the Bedouins and their herds go into the deep desert, but during the dry summer months, they go closer to the cultivated land with its springs and wells.

Yet one must not think that the *Badawi* are not an intelligent people, evidence to the contrary being in how the various tribes are classified according to the animal species which form the basis of their livelihood. First in prestige and importance are the camel nomads, while beneath them rank the sheep and goat wanderers; but no matter the classification of any given group, the head of the family, as well as of each successive social structure is called *shaykh*—the popular "Sheikh" in Western terminology. As to be expected, the *Badawi* are Muslems. In spite of their professed love for Allah, the *Badawi* often break the "rules." Religious traditions, frequently older than the official religion of Islam, play an important role in the *Badawi* life, as do the values of hospitality, bravery, generosity, dignity and honor. Forever they wander, and life goes on . . .

During this July, a tribe of noble *Qaysi Badawi* (which is to say that the members of the tribe could trace their ancestry to northern Arabia) had made its temporary home around the well of Bir El Tamadeh . . . almost two hundred thirty men, women and children, led by *Shaykh* Raouf l'Qaddafi, a desert-hardened man with a long mustache, whose skin had been bronzed the color of mahogany of forty-nine summer suns.

Sitting just within the open flap of his goatskin tent, sipping sweetened black coffee, l'Qaddafi gazed philosophically into the cold night, content with his position in Allah's order of things. Life was good. Life was just, even if the Israelis had made the tribe give up its rifles. l'Qaddafi remembered how the Jews had swept across the Sinai with their armored units in pursuit of the terrified Egyptians.

Shaykh l'Qaddafi did not try to understand such things, although at times he was perplexed as to why Allah had permitted them and their strange god to occupy the land he called home. Indeed, only Allah knew the answer—and the Jews were not a bad people. They never bothered l'Qaddafi and his people, permitting them to live in the manner instilled by centuries of custom.

Pulling his woolen burnoose tighter around him, l'Qaddafi stared out into the night, hearing the wind as it wound its way through the small dunes and pulled gently at the fronds of the palm trees. A small fire burned toward the center of the encampment, around whose flickering flames a group of figures sat huddled.

The sky was clear, the stars as bright as a virgin's glance of anticipation, with only slivers of clouds drifting dreamily across the yellow face of the full moon. Calm was the night . . . the desert Jinns quiet, their moans of evil silent within the wind.

75

Yes, l'Qaddafi considered himself a very fortunate man. His people owned over seventy camels, plus thirty-one goats and sheep, and he himself had three wives and fourteen sons, all growing and healthy sons of Allah. His daughters? l'Qaddafi had not kept track of their number. Why should he? Females were so utterly useless, a shame in the face of any true believer. They were *zewat el-feruj*, good only for the pleasures of the bed, as Allah had ordained. Ahhhh, what more was there to life than the sublime pleasure to be derived from eating meat, riding meat, or pounding meat?

Smiling and picking at his yellowed teeth with the point of a curved dagger which he had taken from his waistband, l'Qaddafi thought of his third wife, whom he had taken in marriage only a few weeks previously. His face hardened then, and the germs of revenge began their sickness in his mind.

"Only thirteen summers old and still a virgin!" her father had told him. "Easily a treasure worth four camels."

Alas, *El-hhemameh*—"The Dove" as she was called—had not been a virgin! By Allah, when l'Qaddafi saw her father again—probably during the winter months—he would demand a return of at least three camels or else taste her father's blood with his dagger. Oh Allah! *El-hhemameh* was still a joy, her almost hairless slit tight and always clinging to his prickle, her passion as demanding and insatiable as her husband's. *Shaykh* l'Qaddafi knew she would bear him many fine sons . . .

Sitting there cross-legged, l'Qaddafi turned and gazed at his sleeping wives and, thinking of The Dove's smooth body, he felt a quickening and a rising of his horn, that horn with which all men buck. The Dove stirred slightly in her sleep, and an old Arab saying sang sweetly in l'Qaddafi's mind— *Suq en-nayk dayim qayim!* By Allah, it was so true—The Tent of Fuck is never struck!

l'Qaddafi decided what he would do. He would awaken The Dove and, together, they would try to strike that tent, for *Buseh bela zubb zay ma'mul bela rubb!*—A kiss without flutter would be as bread without butter . . .

Getting to his feet, l'Qaddafi reached out to close the tent flap. He felt the sensation then . . . the strangeness, the tight tingling in his head, the severe pull and tug as though a dozen devils were twisting and stretching his consciousness. Steadily the brain-shake increased. Alarmed, l'Qaddafi mumbled a prayer to Allah, imploring him to send his protection against the invading demon. Perhaps it was *Ghul,* the mischief maker, or even *El-A'wer,* the evil penis genie and demon of debauchery! Or it could be *El-ghed-dar,* the trickster, or *El-kabus,* the assaulter.

l'Qaddafi looked in alarm at the encampment, where men, women and children were rushing about aimlessly, like lost souls frantically seeking a silent sanctuary! Others were squirming on the ground, or engaged in strange motions and movements . . . a kind of jerking dance without any kind of order or rhythm. Many were screaming at the top of their lungs and clutching at their heads. They yanked off their kaffyehs, then began pawing desperately at their heads, clawing insanely at their hair as if to release the terrible pressure grinding within their brains.

The noiseless, invisible force affected the members of the tribe in various ways, according to their individual personalities. Those whom Allah had cursed with an aggressive disposition became violent . . . murderous . . . in antithesis to those whose natures were cheerful, who began singing and dancing and shouting.

Merrymaking and violent death! One man began strangling his wife! Other men and women battled each other furiously, screaming and howling in madness, slashing at one another with their knives. Blood dripped to the rock and sand, and men, women and children died. Mumbling to herself, one woman flung her infant into the camp fire, then began dancing around the flames as the child, wailing in agony, its flesh frying and sizzling, burned to death.

But none of it mattered to l'Qaddafi, who staggered around and saw that his three wives had awakened. Antima began moaning and pulling at her hair, her fat body swaying. Suddenly, she began to jerk, as if suffering from epilepsy. Anzikor began crawling on all fours, baring her teeth and snapping like a maddened dog.

The Dove pushed back the goat skin cover and, leaping stark naked to her feet, began alternately laughing and crying. Spittle rolled down her chin and her eyes rolled like marbles in her head. She tried to talk, but could only make weird gurgling noises. The psychic earthquake shattering her mind was too great. Nor could l'Qaddafi help her, not that he wanted to, the mental tornado within his own mind having deprived him of his will to act.

The monstrous pressure within his mind increased, the vivid impressions of pain and horror steadily nibbling at his soul and sanity, a knifing from hell that was slicing his brain into numerous parts. Fantastic visions began weaving before his eyes . . . devils and demons and giant exploding stars! A billion voices whispering, taunting him, demanding that he do what they wanted—and why not?

KILL THEM KILL THEM KILL THEM KILL THEM KILLLLLLLLLLL!

A gigantic rage bubbled in l'Qaddafi's distorted mind. Jerking out his dagger, he swayed clumsily toward the Dove—and still the force kept building in his mind, the pressure in his soul increasing as, 82.7 miles away, not too distant from the city of Suez, a tall, thin man, who was worried about his sinus condition, sniffed and turned a large dial, increasing the power of the Psychotron, while standing next to him, a freckled-faced man smiled evilly.

Screaming curses, l'Qaddafi grabbed The Dove by her long inky hair and, with one swift motion, cut the child-bride's throat, giggling as a geyser of blood leaped from her gaping throat. Antima and Anzikor didn't seem to notice. They also died quickly, l'Qaddafi's razor-sharp blade parting the pulsating flesh of their throats.

He stared stupidly down at them, giggling and slobbering . . . now completely insane, so demented that he no longer had enough reason left to know what he had done . . . not even enough sense to kill himself. He didn't have to! The insidious power of the Psychotron did it for him! A massive hemorrhage mushroomed in his mind and his brain exploded, the gray matter wriggling and pushing against the interior of his skull. Still grinning like a homicidal maniac, his wind-blown face twisted like a gargoyle's, *Shaykh* Raouf l'Qaddafi sank to the ground . . . dead . . . blood pouring from his mouth and nose and ears.

Within ten minutes or so, all life had fled from Bir El Tamadeh . . . the corpses of men, women and children scattered about the camp or lying still in goatskin tents. Depending on the individual state of their health, some died sooner than others. But now, all were dead, either by their own hand or by the hands of their demented tribesmen. Or else, like l'Qaddafi, their brains had burst from massive hemorrhage.

The animals were also dead . . . the large pack of camels that had been tethered at one end of the camp, as well as the goats, the sheep and the dogs . . . all lying on the cool sand, growing stiff with the finality of Death.

Bir El Tamedeh had become an instant graveyard.

The Psychotron had done its work well.

CHAPTER VIII

"It's been two weeks, and it would seem that Assad is a man who adheres to a rigid schedule," Richard Camellion said, putting a raisin into his mouth. "He should be leaving the Ministry building in another twenty minutes."

"But will he go to the Amtorg house?" Israela asked.

Disguised as Egyptians, the Death Merchant and Israela Diamant sat in a white Toyota, a quarter of a block from the Ministry of the Interior building in Cairo. With darkened skin and features that had been altered beyond recognition of their real selves, the two Israeli intelligence agents were disguised so perfectly that there was nothing about their appearance that might arouse suspicion, that placed them apart in looks from millions of other Egyptians. This was especially true of Israela, whose dark hair and eyes lent themselves naturally to the concealment of her true identity. With Camellion the task had been more difficult. He had to wear a dark wig. Contact lenses changed the color of his eyes.

"Richard, once we make the attempt and fail—we'll never have another chance to kidnap him! You know that!" Israela said. "He'd be so well guarded that a second try would be out of the question!"

"If we goof it today, we'll never have another opportunity to do anything!" Camellion replied. "We'll be in the next world . . . if there is one . . . which I doubt."

"You don't believe in God?"

Camellion smiled. "If God exists, He must be a practical joker."

Thinking about their mission, Israela said, "We still can't be positive that Assad will go to the Amtorg house this afternoon. Suppose he doesn't—what then?"

"We'll wait until he does," Camellion said. "It's not difficult for our cell to have a second car following us."

"We're still assuming a lot!"

"We have to. You know as well as I do that Assad visits Kagorin every other day," Richard said. "We know that from watching fatso. There's no reason why he should deviate from his schedule today. That's what I like about tubby, he's a creature of habit . . . very, very predictable."

Israela gave him a quick curious glance. What he had said made sense. She couldn't deny that so far all had gone as planned. Smuggling the Death Merchant's makeup equipment into Egypt had been the most difficult phase of the venture —but necessary. Egyptian Customs might have wondered about a tourist who carried a complete theatrical makeup kit around with him! Isser Langbein had taken care of that complicated task—Shin-Bet agents having taken the precious suit-case via a route that included crossing the Red Sea by dhow, over to Egypt, then north by caravan through the Egyptian Arabian Desert; finally the makeup lab had reached the Shin-Bet espionage cell in Cairo's "Old City"—Egyptian Jews who had managed to keep their religious convictions carefully hidden.

The journey that Richard and Israela had taken had been equally as circuitous, an indirect route that took them first to West Berlin where, disguised as German tourists, they next boarded a Lufthansa jet for Paris; then an Air France flight to Cairo, Camellion's left arm strapped tightly to his side, a part of the disguise Langbein had argued against.

"Disguising yourself as a one armed man is too danger-ous," he told Camellion. "In case of trouble, you'd have the use of only one arm."

"Not with the harness I'll be using," Camellion explained. "In case of serious trouble, I can bend my arm at a certain angle and instantly unsnap it. I'm only using this one-arm getup because I want our disguises to be extra special."

They were! When the Death Merchant had finished his handiwork, Richard Camellion and Israela Diamant no longer existed. In their place stood Herr and Frau Emil Schirmer, a German couple in their middle sixties. Emil (a retired postal worker from Steglitz, a section of West Berlin, so his passport stated) had only one arm, was almost bald and sported a well-trimmed but heavy mustache, while Hanna, his wife, was a dumpy, large-breasted woman whose hair appeared plastered to her head, including the large bun in the back. Since she almost waddled when she walked, it was obvious that Frau Schirmer liked large servings of apple strudel.

Taking their first vacation since Emil retired from the postal service, the German couple had no difficulty passing through Egyptian Customs. Playing to the hilt the part of tourists, they excitedly took a cab from the airport and registered at the Hotel des Roses, obtaining a comfortable two-room suite.

In case the Egyptian secret police might be watching them—possible but not probable—for the first four days Camellion and Israela did what all legitimate tourists always do: they busied themselves with Cairo's points of interest, visiting the mosques and rubbernecking in the Tutenkhamon collection of golden furniture in the Egyptian Museum, never for a moment forgetting that they were in the enemy's stronghold.

While it surprised other Westerners with whom the Schirmers came in contact, the fact that there was little talk of war among the Egyptians or that visitors from the West weren't spit on as the "running dogs of Zion-imperialism" didn't astonish the two Shin-Bet agents. Knowing Egyptian emotions as they did, they both realized it was far more characteristic of the Egyptian temperament to welcome the stranger with a soft, friendly and sometimes feckless heart and, above all, to maintain a wise and enlightened air of wry humor and fatalistic indifference amid seemingly final threats and ultimate disasters. Or as Herr Schirmer explained to a visiting college girl from Du Quoin, Illinois, USA, "You must understand, Miss Hunt, that the Egyptians have the ability to separate cosmic and political disagreements from personal endeavors and individual relationships."

"Maybe you're right," Miss Hunt replied, "but it's still darned odd. I thought the Egyptians and the Israelis had a kind of war going! The President of Egypt is always saying how he's going to wipe Israel off the face of the earth! Yet nothing's happening, nothing at all!"

Thinking of their mission, Israela and Camellion exchanged sly glances. Surface appearances were always deceiving. The guns were silent across the Suez, only seventy miles away—except for an occasional shot—now and then one might see Russian military trucks rumbling through Cairo's suburbs. One would almost think the Egyptian people didn't care, although in the coterie of diplomats, journalists and official spokesmen who was the city's nearest thing to an "informed circle," the inevitable question was being constantly asked: would there be another Arab-Israeli war?

The Death Merchant and Israela Diamant knew the answer: Positively!—unless the Death Merchant could find and demolish the Psychotron . . .

The average tourist (or, for that matter, the average Egyptian) knew none of this. For the foreign visitor Cairo was a happy hunting ground of adventure, a virtual gold mine, particularly for those scholars of Islam, to whom its towering minarets and crumbling walls were milestones of history and architecture; but for the ordinary tourist the city's appeal was simply the abundance and intensity of what Egyptians referred to as *baladi*—the "popular life." And as part of their cover, Camellion and Israela tested some of the *baladi*.

They gaped at and commented on the landmarks. They visited the night spots, and on the fifth day they went to where all tourists eventually find themselves: to the Khan el Khalil, or Mousky, one of the most famous bazaars of the Near East, in Cairo's Old City. El Mousky itself was a long narrow street with all sorts of shops pushing a million varieties of specialties and souvenirs—carpets, silks and brocades, perfume, cotton items and leather goods, copper and glass vases, jewelry and what-have-you.

Herr and Frau Schirmer took their time browsing through the various shops on the Khan el Khalil, finally coming to the establishment in which they were the most interested: the shop of Abdul Kariyeh, the Coppersmith—to them the most important spot in Cairo, as it was the headquarters of the Israeli intelligence cell, the unit containing ten members headed by Nasir Gohassin, one of the coppersmiths who worked for Abdul Kariyeh. The Shin-Bet unit had been in operation for seven and a half years.

Quietly, when no other customers were present in the shop, Camellion and Israela disappeared into the back section of the place, where they had a meeting with Gohassin in a tiny underground room beneath the cellar of the shop.

At once, the Death Merchant was relieved to see that his makeup equipment had arrived on schedule, knowing that without it his plans to abduct Egypt's Minister of the Interior could not possibly succeed. It would not be wise to shadow Assad as Westerners; furthermore, makeup was sorely needed to keep up the pretense of German tourists.

Plans were made, with Camellion making it clear that he would make all the decisions, to which Gohassin, having received his orders from Tel-Aviv, readily agreed.

"Israela and I will be disguised as lower class Egyptians,"

83

Camellion said, "and we'll use this secret room as a makeup studio. You're not suspected by the Egyptian secret police are you?"

"God has been good to us," Gohassin replied. "The police don't even know we exist. We have been very cautious all these years—and very lucky."

Camellion surveyed the dimly-lit room. "This room," he said. "It has an atmosphere of absolute finality. Down here we can be absolutely cornered. I don't like it and I don't have your faith in God!"

A small withered old man with long, protruding teeth, Gohassin smiled, "Ah, my American friend," he said—and his English was reasonably good—"necessity is the best teacher one can have, as well as being the mother of all invention."

Getting up, he went over to one wall and pulled down hard on a peg. Silently, a portion of the rough stone wall swung inward, revealing the entrance to a pitch black passageway.

"This leads to the shop of Onnig Hatoun, the rugmaker, five doors down the street," Gohassin said. A happy, almost too happy, smile was on his leathery face. "The passage itself is part of an ancient sewer—or was. It is now dry and forgotten, and we have made good use of it, as you can see."

"Hatoun is a trusted member of your cell?" Israela asked, staring at the old man.

"And an old and dear friend," Gohassin said quietly. "It is he who will dispose of the fat one's worthless body after you bring the Minister here and extract the location of 4-FD from him. With God's help you will succeed in your mission —and for the sake of Israel and the world, you had better!"

I've never seen God fire an UZI!—but Camellion said, "Tell me what you know about Assad. I need information about his personal habits. I also require a detailed map of Cairo."

Confident of their ability, Camellion and Israela returned to the coppersmith's shop the next morning and departed an hour later, leaving by way of Hatoun, the rugmaker's and getting into a Saab parked in the narrow alley behind his place of business. A British Ford slowly started after them, the driver, Nafid Immel, another member of the Cairo Shin-Bet cell.

The surveillance of Hasan El Assad, Minister of the Interior of Egypt, had begun.

Shortly after sunset, Camellion and Israela returned, still disguised as Arabs as they entered the shop of The Rug-maker. An hour and a half later, they left the shop of The Coppersmith, but as Herr and Frau Schirmer, going by way of the front entrance, their arms full of souvenirs.

"By the time this is over, we're going to have enough junk to start a shop of our own!" Israela whispered.

For two weeks they continued their subtle scrutiny of Hasan El Assad, each day using a different make car and each night returning to the Hotel des Roses as the Schirmers.

Finally the Death Merchant was ready and, at a meeting of the Cell, during which time all its member were present, final plans were formulated. Hasan El Assad would be kidnaped one afternoon when he went to visit Colonel Kagorin, the Death Merchant choosing the Amtorg estate on Port Said Street because the location presented the best route for a quick and successful getaway. Traffic was not too heavy in that section of the city, and this sparseness of vehicles would facilitate switching cars, as well as cut down on the number of possible witnesses. More importantly, the nearest police station was almost two and a half miles away.

Israela looked at the wide steps of the Ministry of the Interior building.

"Assad should be putting in an appearance about this time," she said, "unless something's happened to detain him." She tossed the stub of her cigarette out the car window and adjusted her flowing skirt, uncomfortable in the native Egyptian costume, yet far more relaxed than when wearing the padded clothing of "Frau Schirmer."

Without turning his head, Camellion said, "Remember what I told you about being careful not to hit Assad—assuming that he does go to Kagorin's this afternoon. Assad's body-guards will no doubt think it's an assassination attempt and make him lie flat on the floor of the car, so don't fire at the back end."

"I'll keep it in mind," Israela said in annoyance, "After all, I'm not exactly an amateur!" He didn't reply, and she gave him a quick glance, secretly admiring the superb job of disguise he had done, both on her and on himself.

Playing the role of a guide, he was decked out in a red fez, blue woolen *gibba,* an outer coat, and blue figured *gofta,* an inner robe made of silk and cotton; on his right sleeve was an armband which was the guide's ID, his "license" to practice. He didn't mind the Egyptian clothes because they permitted him the use of both arms, unlike "Herr Schirmer" who had to go about with only one arm.

"Assad's limousine has just pulled up," Camellion said.

"I see it," Israela said.

Some five minutes later, they saw the small knot of men walking down the steps of the Ministry building—Assad and his two Egyptian bodyguards. Two other men, Westerners, were with them, stocky men with that well-fed peasant look.

"Ivans!" the Death Merchant said in a flat voice, "and very unfortunate ones at that. This might be their last day of life on this stinking little planet!"

"Ours too!" Israela reminded him.

The five men got into the long gray car—was it a Chrysler? —Camellion couldn't be sure—and the vehicle moved away from the curb, gradually picking up speed and easing its way into traffic.

Keeping well behind it, a Toyota followed.

Neither the Death Merchant nor his assistant spoke, his eyes watching the road and the limousine, hers also riveted to the long gray car half a block ahead of them.

Assad's car turned right on Al Tahrir Street. "They're headed in the right direction," Richard said. "If they turn off on Port Said, we'll know we're in business."

Fifteen minutes later, the Chrysler made a right and turned on Port Said Street.

"This is our Christmas!" Camellion said coldly. "Check the hypo and get the machine guns ready." He was now the pure professional and sounded like it. "You blast the two Ivans at the gate, and I'll take care of the car. If I get hit, don't stop to help—just leave the area as quickly as you can."

"Suppose you only are wounded?"

"Then I'll finish myself off!"

Israela glanced apprehensively at her wrist watch—3:20. Opening the dash compartment, she took out a flat case, opened it, and checked the hypodermic needle: it was ready. Then, kneeling on the seat and turning to face the back, she leaned over and looked at the floor where three UZI machine guns lay wrapped in towels, and a dozen clips, also wrapped.

After transferring guns and clips to the front seat, she quickly unwrapped the weapons and loaded them, finishing the task just as Assad's car entered the block on which the Amtorg house was located.

"Too bad the UZIs don't have silencers," Camellion said lazily. "The noise of gunfire irks me."

A few minutes later, the limousine slowed, then turned onto the short asphalt drive that led to the gates of the elaborately grilled fence surrounding the Amtorg grounds.

Camellion and Israela knew that the next 10 seconds would be moments of extreme danger. NOW!—when the Death Merchant pulled up to the curb, only thirty feet from the Chrysler! NOW!—would Assad's Egyptian bodyguards or the Russians suspect a "hit" and attempt to back the car out of the drive? The Russian gate guards had to be considered. If they should suspect that all was not correct and kept hidden, they could cut the Death Merchant to pieces when he opened fire!

However, Fate is not always fickle. As it turned out, the Russians guarding the gates did not become suspicious nor did the security agents in Assad's car.

The Chrysler stopped in front of the double gates, and instantly the "gate-keepers" appeared and began unlocking them.

The Death Merchant and Israela Diamant went into action!

While Israela poked the snout of an UZI out the window of her side of the Toyota, Camellion leaped to the road, a machine gun in his hands and another UZI slug to his back. *Now I step me out to die!* he thought, and dashed to the long car parked horizontal to the Toyota.

The Russians on the other side of the gate looked at him in surprise, and faces in the car—an Egyptian in the front seat and Assad in the back—looked in his direction, their expressions pure astonishment.

The hammer & sickle slobs, opening the gates, didn't stay surprised very long. They did a dance that would have shamed the most fanatical of whirling dervishes, as Israela sent a stream of burning steel tearing through their bodies, the shrill stacatto of her UZI shattering the quiet afternoon. Even the leaves of the trees lining Port Said Street seemed to jump at the insult of being disturbed by the raucous chatter of her machine gun.

A split second later—even before the racket of Israela's

87

weapon had died away—the Death Merchant cut loose with his machine gun. First he sent half a clip of slugs into the engine of the car, blasting it to junk. Then he turned his weapon on the front seat.

Trying to draw a bead on Camellion with a pistol that resembled a German Luger, the Egyptian bodyguard looked incredibly alarmed when a couple of the Death Merchant's slugs burst his head like an orange that had been stepped on. Instantly he found himself in the Mohammedan version of heaven, ogling the virgin *Houris* and wondering how in hell he had gotten there! Back on earth, his body fell forward, slumping against the dash of the car.

Sitting next to the now-corpse of the bodyguard, the Egyptian chauffeur died just as quickly, finding it impossible to live with four of Camellion's slugs in his neck and head. The first of the blast knocked him against the door, causing his elbow to strike the handle. The door opened and, like a sack of wet cement, the chauffeur slid to the hot sticky asphalt of the drive, a pool of red widening beneath him.

"ASSAD! KEEP DOWN! KEEP DOWN!" a voice from the back seat shouted.

Dropping very low, beyond the range of the men in the back seat—unless they exposed themselves—the Death Merchant raced behind the car, coming up on the opposite side, just as the rear door opened and a Russian, his head low and a .43 caliber Zortov pistol in his hand, began crawling out.

He glanced up at the Death Merchant—then stared straight into the mystery of eternity while the merchant of a sudden and violent demise blew his head off, the power of the slugs slamming him to the drive and pitching him almost on top of of the chauffeur. The Ivan lay there like a giant, crumpled doll, his sightless eyes staring up at the boiling Egyptian sun.

What were the other Russian and the Egyptian in the back seat doing? Although Camellion wasn't too concerned about Assad, who was hunched down in the right hand corner of the back seat, Richard was only too conscious of the fact that a trapped animal often puts up a vicious battle.

Assad might be a coward! the voice of logic whispered to Camellion. *If he comes up shooting, you might have to kill him to save your own life! But how to waste the Russian and the Egyptian? Why not blast them through the back window!*

Hearing the rear door on the opposite side opening, Camellion began easing toward the left hand corner of the vehicle;

that's when Israela's UZI began its rapid snarl of death. The Egyptian, whose fear had foolishly forced him to expose himself by leaving the car, was now paying the price. He jerked violently, as if having an epileptic seizure, and died like the dummy he was . . . riddled with slugs. The revolver fell from his cooling fingers and, sliding against the car, he flowed to the drive and lay still.

I hope Israela's slugs didn't hit Assad! Raising his body slightly, the Death Merchant peeked around the left side of the car's rear window—ducked, turned his head and closed his eyes, just in time to miss the hot slice of slugs from the remaining Ivan's machine pistol! The back window dissolved, and the Death Merchant dropped down to the left rear wheel of the car. He unslung his other UZI. Precious time was being lost. The Russian couldn't get at him, but neither could he see the Russian! Camellion knew he had to divert the man's attention—he did so by triggering a long burst of slugs at one of the iron posts supporting the gate, in front of the car. Three of the slugs, after striking the post, zinged into the front windshield, instantly turning the glass into a spiderweb pattern of crazy cracks.

Now or not at all! Leaping to the left side of the limousine, his blue *gibba* flopping, Camellion stared through the open door and saw that the Russian, crouched on the floor, was staring up at the cracked windshield. The man's startled face jerked toward Camellion, and that was the last thing Stephen Zhilin saw—and felt—in this world: the black muzzle of an UZI machine gun and—but for a tiny spit in time—the unbelievable pain of a half dozen slugs chopping into his broad Slavic chest. He blinked, fell back, died.

The rear of the car contained a long back seat and, on each side, a short one. Hasan El Assad was crouched in front of the long seat, on the floor, next to the dead Russian. An obese man, dressed in a brown silk suit, he shook with fright. He reminded Camellion of an overgrown slug. Turning his head, he looked up at the Death Merchant. "P-Please," he said, his voice a roller-coaster of fear, "don't—don't kill me!"

"Then move right now and move fast, or I will!" Camellion hissed, poking him in the leg with the barrel of the UZI.

Assad instantly obeyed, and began easing his corpulent bulk from the car. His bald head was covered with a tidal wave of sweat and the muscles of his cheeks jerked uncontrollably from fear.

"Run to that Toyota over there," Camellion ordered as they crouched by the side of the car. "Try to escape, and I'll blow you apart!"

Standing erect, the Death Merchant glanced toward the Amtorg house—and saw the face looking at him around a *meshrebiya,* the intricate wooden screen covering a second floor harem-shaped window.

The man was Constantine Alexis Kagorin.

At 3:00 that afternoon, Colonel Kagorin sat discussing the situation with N. G. Merkulov, who was no longer posing as John Cecil Evers, and with two of the SMERSH assassination specialists who had arrived recently from Moscow. Paul Klopkov was also in the room.

'I'm not going to take the slightest chance with the Death Merchant," Kagorin said. "Not the slightest! If any of our men survived the Jerusalem massacre, you can bet all the vodka you'll ever drink that the Death Merchant will make them talk!"

Merkulov shrugged. "So what if Camellion does! None of them know the location of the Psychotron complex. They can't tell him what they don't know!"

Kagorin shot Merkulov a look that would have withered a zombie. "You're missing the point," the GRU chief snapped. "If one of our agents was captured and has the idea that Assad knows the location . . . if he should tell that to those Shin-Bet bastards, you can damn well be certain that the Death Merchant will be coming after Assad. That's the *way* he operates!"

Smoking a fat cigar, Valdimir Vensensky, one of the SMERSH specialists, blew out a thick cloud of smoke. Kagorin glanced in annoyance at him—didn't the man ever inhale? "I was under the impression that Assad was ignorant of the Psychotron," Vensensky said. A huge man, tall and broad, he had a horse face and teeth to match.

"Assad—that bourgeoise imbecile!" sneered Kagorin. "He only knows the location of what he presumes to be a weather station, but if the Shin-Bet and Camellion get wise to the fact that this station is really the Psychotron complex and that Assad knows its location—do you see the danger? That damned Camellion! He's always thinking ahead of next week!"

90

"I assume that's why you sent the other two SMERSH experts to pick up Assad this afternoon," Klopkov said. "Myself, I can't possibly conceive even the Death Merchant trying to kidnap Assad. That's what he'd have to do to get any information from him!"

"I can conceive it!" growled Kagorin, looking at his pocket watch, "and that's exactly why I sent Monastyriskii and Lipalo to protect him." He looked at his watch again. "They should be arriving any moment with the fat fool. I want to tell him that—"

The snarl of a machine gun startled Kagorin to the extent that he almost dropped his watch. Automatically, as trained as they were, the Russians dropped to the thick Persian rug, including Kagorin, who along with the others began crawling toward the windows. Cautiously, he peered over the edge—and cursed. An Egyptian woman had just machine gunned the two gate guards—goddam the dirty bitch!—and another Egyptian, this one a man, was slamming slugs into the engine of Assad's official car.

Kagorin screamed at Paul Klopkov, "CALL THE POLICE. TELL THEM THEIR MINISTER OF THE INTERIOR IS BEING ASSASSINATED!" Then he snarled at Valdimir Vensensky and the other murder-specialist, "Get out there, you idiots! Assad may already be dead!"

The two SMERSH agents crawled across the room, reached up, opened the door, and crawled through the opening.

Kagorin continued to crouch on the floor, cursing and listening to the firing, which continued for two or three minutes. Then silence! He stood up by the side of one window and looked around the edge, staring through the wooden-grilled screen. He cursed again and literally shook in hatred and frustration. There, standing by the bullet-riddled gray car, looking up at him, was the Egyptian! Kagorin wasn't fooled. The son of a bitch had to be the Death Merchant! Who else but Richard Camellion would have the nerve to attack the Minister of the Interior—and right in front of the Amtorg estate, which any intelligent person realized was the home base of the Russian secret police in Egypt.

The Russian colonel jerked his head back, and a vicious rain of UZI slugs tore through the wooden screen. There was a popping sound, the destructive tinkle of glass and metal being shattered. Kagorin stared across the room. The machine

91

gun slugs had completely destroyed three of his clocks resting on the mantle.

Kagorin almost vomited. One of the clocks had been a marble and bronze antique, made in France over 200 years ago!

The Death Merchant prodded Hassan El Assad into the back seat of the Toyota, and even as Camellion slammed the door, Israela was turning the car on to Port Said Street, ignoring the other cars that, for a time, slowed to see what the excitement was all about. Camellion grinned! His slugs had come so close to Kagorin! Only "close" wasn't good enough.

Glancing through the back window of the car, Richard saw two men running down the long drive toward the Chrysler. Firing over Assad, who was crouched on the floor, Camellion had the satisfaction of seeing one of the Ruskies go down, but he had missed the other man, who flung himself sideways to the grass. Then the men were out of sight as Israela fed gas to the souped-up engine.

She reached into the dash, took out the hypodermic kit and passed it back to the Death Merchant.

"We'll wait until we make the transfer," Richard said. "This ton of blubber is too heavy to carry, and we'd lose too much time by putting him under now. Besides, we're not going to have any trouble with him—are we?" He pressed the muzzle of the UZI into Assad's fat neck.

"Think we'll make it?" Israela asked. Her voice was very calm.

"We're dead if we don't!" Camellion answered. "If Nafid's late with the truck, we've had it. In a very short while, the Egyptian police will have this license number."

Five minutes more and Israela was turning off Port Said onto Al Qalaa. Another seven minutes and they were pulling up behind an unmarked step-in van, the kind used for shop deliveries.

Once more Assad felt the muzzle of the UZI on his neck. "We're going to leave the car and walk into that van. Try to run or call out and I'll kill you."

The transfer from Toyota to van took only a minute, even though they deliberately walked nonchalantly, to fool anyone who might be looking their way. The van pulled away from

92

the curb as Camellion plunged the hypodermic needle into Assad's arm, sending the man into instant unconsciousness. On Bir Nidda, after spotting two police cars racing in the opposite direction, they turned off into that section that led to the Old City. A short time later the van stopped in the alley behind the rugmaker's shop on Khan el Khalil. Passing Arabs in the alley didn't give the van a second glance. There was nothing unusual about three of their kind carrying a large bundle of rolled-up rugs into a rugmaker's shop.

Another ten minutes, and Hasan El Assad was in the secret room beneath the cellar of Abdul Kariyeh's establishment.

The hypo that Camellion had given Assad had been a mild one, and after a counteractive had been administered to the man, while they were waiting for him to revive, Camellion changed himself and Israela back into Herr and Frau Schirmer.

Nasir Gohassin watched Israela filling another hypodermic. "Pentothal?" he exclaimed. "On top of a knock-out solution? My friends, are we not tweaking the nose of fate? Assad has a heart condition."

"But a mild heart condition," Camellion said, "and we have no choice. We can't depend solely on what he might consciously tell us."

Regaining consciousness, Assad sat up on the cot and stared around him, looking first in fear at Gohassin, then at the two persons whom he did not, at first, associate with his abduction. Then he guessed who Camellion really was! "You're the Death Merchant!" he said in broken English. "Colonel Kagorin has spoken about you many times!"

"Get up, Assad, and sit in that chair," Camellion said, indicating a chair by the table. "Be a good boy and we won't handcuff you."

Assad's eyes fastened on the hypodermic in Frau Schirmer's hand. "W-What is that?" he asked, his voice quivering. He moved slowly to the chair and sat down. "What are you going to do to me?"

"Pentothal," Israela said. "We need information and you're going to give it to us! But don't worry"—and she spoke in Egyptian—"*bukra fil mish-mish,*" and jabbed the needle into his fat arm.

The Death Merchant glanced at Gohassin, asking him with

an inquiring look what Israela had said. Gohassin smiled. " 'Tomorrow the apricots will bloom,' " he explained. "An ancient Egyptian proverb, similar to your 'tomorrow will be better.' "

Under the influence of sodium pentothal, Assad told them what they wanted to know—almost. Yes . . . he knew the location of Meteorological Station 4-FD, the only one the Russians were operating. Station 4-FD was not far from the city of Suez, about ten miles or so to the northwest. A—Psychotron? No . . . Assad didn't know anything about such a device. Could he point out the 4-FD complex on the map? Yes, he thought so, but he wasn't positive. He was not an expert with maps.

They continued to question Assad after the twilight effect of the truth drug had worn off, but made no reference to the Mind Blaster. At first, Assad tried to pretend he was brave and refused to answer their questions.

"I have no intention of cooperating with you!" he said, almost stuttering in his apprehension. He rubbed his arm where the hypodermic needle had pierced the skin. His white shirt was sweat-plastered to his body. "After the next war, there will be no Israel and the capitalists in the United States will regret that—"

His large eyes bugged, and his mouth fell open, moving like a fish's as Camellion put the muzzle of a silenced Beretta Brigadier to his head.

"Listen, stupid," Camellion said in a very serious voice, "you'll either point out the location of the weather station or you'll die very slowly and very painfully. Do you know how long it takes to die with a slug in the belly?"

Assad's breathing became very labored . . . his chest rising and falling rapidly.

Camellion's gaze went to Israela, whose face was without expression. They both realized that Assad was a doomed man, that there was no possible way they could permit him to live. He knew too much. He had to die. It was that simple. The catch was, did Assad know it? He probably tried not to think about it, because while Hope creates strength of will, it can also warp judgment and reality.

"But before you die, my weighty friend, you will receive a taste of this!" Gohassin said mildly, showing Assad a piece of rope whose length contained two large knots. Quickly he stepped behind the Egyptian Minister and flung the rope around his head in such a way that the two knots rested on Assad's eyes.

"Ahhhh, my fat one, can you guess what the knots will do when the rope is tightened?" Gohassin asked. "Your eyeballs will pop like two grapes."

"He should know," Israela said bitterly. "Egyptian soldiers used the eye crusher on Israeli prisoners during the war, not to mention castration and the hacking off of hands and feet. Or have you conveniently forgotten, Mr. Minister of the Interior?"

Assad made a gurgling sound when Gohassin began tightening the rope, and he made a noise like a squawking chicken when the knots began pressing against his eyelids.

"I-I'll do it!" he screamed, rising from his chair. "I'll show you on the map!"

Assad did just that—bent over the table on which rested a large map of Egypt, his stubby finger resting on a point not far from Suez. Camellion took down the coordinates.

"I think he's lying," Israela said. She picked up a Beretta and pulled back the slide, cocking it. "I think we should kill him right now!"

Assad began thumping his finger on the map. "4-FD is about here," he said in a choked voice, "just where I said it was. But I keep telling you, this complex is only a weather station. I should know! I've inspected the place at least a half dozen times, as part of my official duties. Right there— that's where it is."

"And you saw exactly what Colonel Kagorin wanted you to see," Camellion said softly. "He made a fool of you, Assad."

Realization began glowing in Assad's eyes, the awareness that the weather station was only a cover for something far more important. He sighed, "So, just as I suspected. That Russian clock-maker lied to me!"

" 'Clock-maker!' " Israela exclaimed. "Kagorin?"

"Kagorin's hobby," Camellion said, his eyes never leaving Assad.

"I always suspected they were hiding something at that weather station, but I could never prove it," Assad said. "That explains why the base is always so well guarded. I could never understand that; now it makes sense."

Suddenly, he realized what he had just revealed and clamped his mouth shut.

95

"How well guarded?" Camellion asked. "How many men?"

"What kind of armament?" Gohassin asked.

Assad hesitated. He glanced fearfully at the rope dangling from Gohassin's hand.

"I don't know," Assad replied in a pitiful voice. He sounded as if he might break down and cry. "At least twenty-five of our people are there, and . . . and perhaps a hundred or so Russians . . . and maybe a dozen tanks."

"What kind of tanks?" Israela asked.

"Mediums. Russian T-54s."

"Missiles?" probed Camellion.

"None that I know of," Assad replied, wiping rivers of sweat from his face.

Camellion smiled sinisterly. "No, I don't suppose they would have missiles. Missiles at a weather station. Even *you* would have been suspicious of that!"

"Missile sites are also difficult to camouflage from the air," Israela said.

"Assad, listen to me," Camellion said, "we're keeping you here until we've checked out what you've told us. If you've lied, you're going to wish you were dead—and you'll be wishing that for a week before you do meet your ancestors!"

The Death Merchant knew that Assad could not have lied under the spell of pentothal. But conscious? Had he lied about the coordinates on the map? The Death Merchant didn't think so. The man was too terrified . . . too afraid of death.

Assad's face twisted with the dread of dying. He put his finger on the map again. "I tell you, the base is here, right here," he said. "I swear it. See—see this line here. This is the road from Suez that leads out into the desert. You turn off about here, give or take a mile or more, and about here— this is the weather station . . . right in this area. I might be off a mile or more. I—I'm not an expert with maps."

"If the station is in the general area, we'll find it," Camellion said. Deciding to be merciful to Assad, Camellion was letting the idea of shooting him in the back of the head tumble around in his mind, when blubber gut least expected it. The poor man would be dead before he realized his heart had stopped beating.

He was about to walk around Assad and raise his Beretta when he noticed a small red light flashing above the telephone that rested across the room on a small shelf. Gohassin also saw the danger warning and, as he picked up the phone, a look of extreme apprehension flashed across his swarthy face, deepening when he heard the news.

"How near the shop are they?" he said into the phone. "No, of course not. There can be no surrender."

Sensitive to the breath of Death, Camellion and Israela knew the Egyptian police were closing in. Why or how the police had traced Assad didn't matter. Someone had probably witnessed the transfer from Toyota to van and taken down the van's license number. The police had then traced the van to its owner—Abdul Kariyeh, the coppersmith, under whose shop the Minister of the Interior was now a prisoner.

Gohassin returned the phone to its cradle. "Abdul said the police are parked across the street, staring at the shop," he said. "Abdul and the two clerks will fight it out. Once the police find out we're Jews . . . ah . . . need I say more, my friends?"

With a look of triumph in his beady eyes, Assad turned to his three captors.

"You see! I knew they would come for me!" he said loudly. "Surrender to me and I will do all I can to have my government spare your lives."

The three Shin-Bet agents ignored the almost strutting Minister of the Interior.

"You two have the required information," Gohassin said to Camellion and Israela. "Go now by way of the sewer passage and take the location of the Mind Blaster base to our people in Tel-Aviv. Unless the Psychotron is smashed, Israel and the free world will become obsolete! Go—quickly, my friends!"

With more hope than sense, and expecting to be freed soon, Assad became demanding. "This talk of a 'Mind Blaster!' What does it mean? Enough of this nonsense! I demand that you release me at once!"

Irked because he was being ignored, Assad decided to show these Jews he was boss. He suddenly called out in a loud voice, "I AM HASAN EL ASSAD, THE MINISTER OF THE INTERIOR OF EGYPT. POLICE! I AM DOWN HERE!"

The Death Merchant's fist lashed out, connecting with Assad's jaw and knocking the man to the floor. Assad stared up at him, disbelief turning his face into a frozen mask.

Pointing his weapon at Assad, Camellion said softly, "If you as much as whisper, I'll kill you."

97

Israela clutched Gohassin by the arm. "Nasir, what about you?" she asked. "What will you do?"

He let his eyes move slowly upward, as if expecting the police to fall through the ceiling, and smiled. "Death holds no terror for me," he said, "not after seventy-three years' existence. I shall remain here"—he glanced at the astonished Assad—"with 'my' Minister. Assad and I shall meet Death together."

Afraid to get to his feet lest the Death Merchant kill him, Assad realized with a sickening horror that this room was to be his tomb—not as fancy as a Pharaoh's, but every bit as effective. He was positive he was almost in the Hereafter when Nasir Gohassin went to a cabinet, opened the top double doors and took down a large box, which he put on the table. Opening the wooden box, he removed a timer-detonator, one whose wires led back into the box.

"Two dozen TNT packs," Nasir said simply. "It will take the police—oh, with luck they should find this place in about fifteen minutes. When they do, I'll turn the timer—poof! No more police! No more Gohassin! No more Minister of the Interior!"

They heard the familiar sounds from upstairs. Machine gun fire! The police were attacking the shop. The beginning of a battle in which the Shin-Bet had to lose.

Drawing a German Mauser from his waist band, Gohassin walked over to the wall peg and pulled it downward. The door to the passageway swung open. Israela took a pencil-flashlight from her purse and snapped it on.

Thumbing off the safety of the Beretta, Richard Camellion turned his attention to Assad, who was blubbering and crying on the floor, the terror of Death having reduced the man to a quivering mass of jelly.

"NO!" Nasier said firmly, pushing Camellion's gun arm to one side. "Don't kill him. Let him wait for the end with me and dwell upon his misdeeds. Now GO! There is no more time."

Still another burst of gunfire from upstairs . . . the deep cough of Egyptian tommy guns . . . the lighter, faster snarl of UZIs. Abdul and his clerks were putting up a good fight, yet one that could only end with their deaths—*Jock would probably call it 'a bloody good show!'*

Israela looked deeply into Nasir's tired old eyes. *"Shalom,"* she said.

"Shalom," he replied.

Without another word, she stepped into the dark passageway. Camellion followed her. "Richard," she said in a low voice, "don't forget to strap down your arm."

The Death Merchant turned to Nasir and shook his hand.

"Goodbye, dear friend," Nasir said, and pulled down on the wall-peg.

Silently the portions of stone swung shut.

No one noticed the Western couple leaving the rugmaker's shop. Since the gunfire had stopped and there was no more danger from flying bullets, a large crowd of onlookers had gathered in front of Abdul Kariyeh's place of business. Five Egyptian police cars were parked across the street.

Moving leisurely, Herr & Frau Schirmer walked in the opposite direction, turning the first corner they came to.

They were a block from Kariyeh's shop when Israela whispered, "The passageway! If the police find it?"

"They won't," Camellion whispered back. "Even if they find the secret room, the explosion is almost certain to seal the passageway. If it doesn't, Hatoun and the others have already left the shop. Hatoun's safe enough for the time being —but do you hear it?"

"What?"

"The rustle of angel feathers!"

They both heard something else then—a tremendous explosion!

Neither commented. The echo of the exploded TNT packs was a speech in itself!

An hour later, Herr and Frau Schirmer walked into the lobby of the Hotel des Roses . . .

Two days later, Herr and Frau Schirmer were on a Lufthansa flight, on their way to West Germany.

Camellion knew that Death rode with them.

CHAPTER IX

Amid an atmosphere of gloom so oppressive that one could almost see it dripping from the walls and ceiling—for the catastrophe at Bir El Tamadeh had eaten holes in the fabric of their confidence—they gathered in a large room on the fifth floor of Tel-Aviv's Town Hall building . . . seven of them, to plot the Commando raid on the Russian Mind Blaster base.

Misha Duryan, Israel's Minister of Defense, adjusted the black patch over his right eye, and then, getting to his feet, leaned over the long conference table, putting his hands flat on the large map, while, with his one good eye, he studied the area around Ayun Mussa, an Arab village of the Sinai that was only 7.5 miles from the city of Suez, the latter of which lay in Egypt to the northwest, directly across the southern section of the Suez Canal.

"Ben, do you feel that five planes will be sufficient for the attack?" Duryan asked, raising his head to Benjamin Bar-Sakol, the Commanding General of the Israeli Air Force, who was seated across the table from him. Richard Camellion was on Bar-Sakol's left, Simon Avidan to the IAF general's right.

"Two Vatour bombers and three Mystère fighters should do the job," Bar-Sakol replied, without looking up from the large aerial photograph he was scrutinizing through a large magnifying glass. "As the plan stands now, we'll saturate the entire area with napalm and phosphorous bombs before Camellion and the Commandos attack. Camellion and his men will finish the attack, successfully it is hoped!"

He put down the magnifier and turned his attention to Richard Camellion, his dull, mournful eyes suggesting a constant and tormenting strain that could not be eased. "You know, Camellion," he said pointedly, "you know that once you and the Commandos go in, you're on your own. You'll have only one chance of getting back to safety—the helicopter. Should it be destroyed . . ."

The Death Merchant picked up an aerial photograph that had been made the day before and looked at it, at the grooves and ridges and the ever so faint rings of tiny circles surrounding the general area—missiles!

Camellion pointed at the missile sites on the photograph. "What about these, if they are missiles?"

Misha Duryan said, "The photographs were taken with high resolution cameras, and I don't think the interpretation of our experts is incorrect. The Russian base is guarded by missiles, probably truck-mounted S-77s. The Ivans haven't had the time to install SA-2s or SA-3s!"

"How can you be so sure, sir?" spoke up Israela, sitting next to Simon Avidan, her long hair tumbling about her shoulders. Dressed in blouse and shorts, she was a very attractive young woman, but no one seemed to notice.

Bar-Sakol sighed, then remembered that Israela and the others were not familiar with the intricacies of aerial photography and the interpretation of aerial photographs.

"The answer is very simple," he said, "We've photographed that section before, as a matter of routine, to check on Egyptian troop concentrations, but it wasn't until after you and Camellion returned from Egypt and told us that the Psychotron base might be in that area that we surveyed it with high resolution cameras. As far as I'm concerned, that's your blaster base. That's your target—well camouflaged, but it's there, nevertheless."

Israela was persistent. "That doesn't explain the missiles, General."

"I'm coming to that," Bar-Sakol replied, his voice very patient. "You and Camellion returned four days ago. The day after you returned, we sent an aircraft over to photograph the entire area you pinpointed. The missiles weren't there then. In fact, we didn't spot them until yesterday, indicative that they had been deployed to that locale within the last several days. Because of the time factor, they had to be trucked in from Suez. That's why Misha said they almost have to be S-77s."

Isser Lev Langbein was watching Bar-Sakol's face intently. "Won't missiles increase the risk factor to our planes?" he asked.

Bar-Sakol pursed his lips. "Ordinarily, yes," he explained. "But not in this case. Our planes will go in low, at minimum level, at about one hundred feet, too low for the missiles to be effective. But anti-aircraft guns are another matter. We're hoping they won't depress that low."

He picked up one of the photographs and pointed to numerous "Xs" ringing the area. "Here and here and here," he said. "Of course, napalm may knock them out with the first strike— and the tanks too. We feel there are at least a dozen Russian mediums in the base area."

Expectantly his gaze swept the table, and he began sucking in on one corner of his lower lip.

Jock Heydecker leaned forward and folded his arms on the table, his sun-tanned face anxious. "We can be positive of one thing," he said. "Kagorin surely knows why Camellion grabbed Assad. Right now he's assuming we're going to hit the weather station with everything we've got. I only hope he doesn't 'ave a squadron of MIGS standing by!"

"He can't." Duryan said with a low chuckle. With an unconscious motion he touched his eye patch. "There's no airfield even close to the Mind Blaster area, nothing but desert . . . rock and sand. We've nothing to worry about on that score."

"But there's plenty to worry about in Suez," Richard Camellion said. Putting down the photograph he'd been studying, he shifted his attention to Langbein, the chief of Israeli Intelligence. "Isser, do you have any information on the number of troops in Suez? We seem to have forgotten that Suez is only some 13 to 14 miles from the Russian base, and it doesn't take long for a company of soldiers to cover that short distance."

"It does if the road they have to travel is blasted all over the face of the map!" Duryan said. "The initial air strike also includes hitting the road, doesn't it, Ben?"

"It had better!" Langbein said. "There are more than 25,000 soldiers in the Suez area . . ."

"About here," Bar-Sakol said. "About here, in this section, we'll blast the road in a dozen or more spots." His finger moved along a green line on the map, and he waited for them to absorb the position before continuing. "With the road destroyed in these spots, it should take any help from Suez at least several hours to reach the Psychotron area." He stared at the Death Merchant. "If your attack's not completed by then, we'll have to mark you off as lost."

Richard grinned. "If we don't succeed within a half hour, we're dead!"

"Camellion, earlier you mentioned a copter to be used as a decoy," Langbein said. "Is that still part of your plan?"

The Death Merchant spoke to Bar-Sakol directly. "I'll have to have three helicopters," he said. "To use only one would be ridiculous. Two would be half-stupid!"

Wearing a brown Israeli Army shirt with double patch pockets, he removed a box of raisins from one pocket and began opening it.

Bar-Sakol shifted in his chair, a movement indicating displeasure. "You're taking only twenty Commandos, Camellion. You and Israela—and I don't believe she should go—and the pilot."

"Correction—two pilots for the main craft!" Camellion said.

"We've been all through that!" Israela flared. "I speak Egyptian and can be of definite help, and I also understand Russian!"

Bar-Sakol ignored the double interruption. "Very well, Camellion! You and Israela and two pilots will make twenty-four! One troop-carrying helicopter will be more than sufficient!"

"That's very correct, as far as troop space only is concerned," Richard said easily, "but suppose that single whirley-bird is damaged on the way over? We'll be going in at ground zero to fool radar and taking a route that offers the least fire from the ground, but that's still no guarantee that the Egyptians won't be throwing flak and everything else at us! One copter just won't cut the mustard!"

"I doubt if one copter would furnish even the bread!" Jock said in a low voice, as if talking to himself.

Giving him an angry glance, Bar-Sakol said to Camellion, "Damn it, man! We've only thirty-five helicopters in the entire Israeli Air Force, and only seventeen are troop carriers! Yet you expect me to risk three of them! You seem to forget that we're a small nation and surrounded by a hundred million Arabs."

The Death Merchant sat thinking, his eyes looking at the two photographs on the opposite wall, one of David Ben-Gurion, the first Prime Minister of Israel, the other of Golda Meir, the present Prime Minister.

"I need three copters," Camellion said. "Two won't do the job."

"Why three, Camellion?" Misha Duryan asked in an almost cheerful voice. He lit a cigarette and inhaled deeply, then removed it from his mouth and looked thoughtfully at it.

103

"One copter as a decoy, to fly in one hundred yards ahead of us. One to carry us and the Commandos, and one as a stand-by, in case ours is damaged to the extent we have to land," Camellion said.

Concentrating on the coming attack, his mind racing far ahead of the others in the room, the Death Merchant felt the present falling away from him. He was no longer sitting among men trying to save their country, but standing amidst fantastic memories . . . talking to men—and the girl—who had become his friends in absentia, in the darkness of nights they had spent as slaves . . . nights before Israel had gained her independence.

Duryan replied, "Sounds like good strategy to me, Richard. Ben, give him the three helicopters. If he doesn't succeed in smashing the Mind Blaster, we won't even have an air force to worry about."

"Huh! We won't even 'ave a country!" Jock said, chomping down on his unlit cigar. "Hell, there's not much point in getting to the base if we can't get back—I mean, if we manage to get our hands on Popvikin, provided he's still at the weather station."

"If Popvikin isn't there?" Simon Avidan asked, directing his question to Camellion.

"Then I'll have to hunt him down in the Soviet Union," the Death Merchant replied. "However, I'm not too concerned about Popvikin not being at the station. What happened at Bir El Tamadeh is very good evidence that Popvikin is still working in the Egyptian desert. I'm convinced he's still at station 4-FD!"

A curious glint flared in Duryan's one good eye. "Explain your reasoning. I don't think I follow you."

"Isn't it fact that in order to waste Bir El Tamadeh the range of the Psychotron had to be increased? Bir El Tamadeh is forty miles further inland than Bel Sida, the first village that was destroyed."

No one said a word. The Death Merchant continued. "As I see it, the Ruskies aren't going to conclude their tests with an insignificant village out in the middle of nowhere. The next logical step will be to increase the range to take in an entire city, and to do that, Popvikin has to remain at 4-FD. Another obvious fact is that the range, as yet, has not been increased—or the people of Tel-Aviv or Haifa might now all be dead . . . or stark raving mad!"

104

"Jesus Christ! That's one hell of a thought!" Jock said in alarm.

"Jock, you've got the wrong god!" Israela said, smiling.

"The Russians could move the Psychotron base!" Simon Avidan said.

Camellion shook his head. "They could . . . if they had the time . . . which they haven't. Look at the situation logically: Kagorin knows we'll strike with all possible speed. He also realizes that his only chance is to speed up work out in the desert and to protect the base with everything he has. He has no other choice. But make no mistake about it—Colonel Kagorin will be expecting us." He looked directly at Misha Duryan, the Minister of Defense. "That's why I want commandos who aren't family men. It's possible that none of us will be coming back. But if we blow up the Psychotron and kill Popvikin, the mission will be a success."

"Well now, that's a truly 'joyful' outlook you have, Camellion!" Duryan joked, giving out with a rolling belly laugh. "If you do get killed in the raid, at least you won't be disappointed."

There was something about Duryan, a quality of independence, of courage, which had a tendency to give those around him an emotional shot of new hope. Duryan could annihilate fatigue and depression with his high, sarcastic laugh, dispel a sentimental mood with an almost ruthless joke and yet create warmth not by laughing or joking, but simply by listening quietly and attentively with a wise, sad smile.

All during the meeting, the Defense Minister had been trying to find a parallel between the coming raid into Egypt and the June 1967 Arab-Israeli War. There was none. The two situations were entirely different. Back in 1967, there were various reasons why Israel defeated numerically superior Arab forces. Shin-Bet intelligence had enabled Israel to seek out vital targets, especially enemy airfields. Also, Israel's high command was tightly organized, a single roomful of officers working under General Rabin. Just as importantly, Israel was a nation united and fighting for its very existence, in contrast to Arab inefficiency and internal distrust.

As for the present situation, there was another ingredient that made it just more than a little sensitive: the fact that the United States had a complicated plan for reopening the

105

Suez Canal and was trying to arrange talks between the Israelis and the Egyptians.

Duryan knew that at this very moment, Yitki Robitz, the Israel Ambassador to the U.S., might be meeting with Franklin W. Burnis, the U.S. Assistant Secretary of State for the Middle East, in an attempt to smooth out the technical difficulties.

Would the Egyptians use the raid for propaganda purposes, as an excuse to accuse Israel of sabotaging the talks before they had even begun? They certainly would, but only if the raid *failed*, if Camellion and the Commandos were wiped out before they could destroy Weather Station 4-FD. If the raid succeeded, the Egyptians would keep their mouths shut, not wanting the world to know that Israeli Commandos had smashed a secret Russian installation housing a weapon responsible for murdering hundreds of innocent Arabs in the Sinai! Even Egypt's Arab allies would take a dim view of that.

Still another factor to the Psychotron raid: The Death Merchant and the Commandos would not be fighting only Egyptians, but also soldiers and specialists of the Soviet Union.

"Yes Camellion . . . a real joyful outlook," Duryan said again. "You'll probably be whistling the 'Star Spangled Banner' when you die."

"Yet my outlook is practical," Camellion replied, "not that I'm planning on committing suicide, but when you play cards with the devil you had better be prepared to lose."

"I hope you bring back at least one helicopter!" Bar-Sakol said, smiling slightly.

Jock Heydecker lit his cigar absent-mindedly. One good thing about the raid, he reminded himself, if it didn't succeed he wouldn't have to worry about the ailments of old age. And somehow this seemed an achievement worth all the trouble of getting his butt shot off. You're bloody well right! We all die, sooner or later, only some die sooner than others.

Looking seriously at the Death Merchant, Duryan stood up and tapped his finger on the map-dot that was Ayun Mussa. "Camellion, I assume you still intend using this village as a hopping-off point. Well, Ayun Mussa is a good choice."

"Give us the plan once more, step by step," Bar-Sakol said.

"We attack tomorrow night," Camellion said. "As they say in Texas, when you have a good horse, ride him double! That's what we're going to do! We'll assemble our forces at Ayun Mussa and—"

CHAPTER X

Dying for the day, the sun had almost crawled down below the horizon, the last of its radiance illuminating the desert with an eerie blanket of orangy-red.

Dressed in a brown short-sleeved shirt and shorts, with his hairy legs spread defiantly, Colonel Alexis Kagorin stood almost in the center of the compound, surveying the sand-colored buildings. His mouth twisted—let the Death Merchant and his Jews attack! They'd find a most welcome reception, one of fire and steel. They'd find only disappointment and quick death.

Like a hawk surveying its surroundings, the GRU Colonel took in every minute detail of the Psychotron base. The three barracks were in front of him, to his left—two for the Russian infantry unit and one for the fifteen Egyptians at the complex.

Across from the barracks was the dispensary and, next to it, the low, flat building, partially underground, that housed the twin generators for surface power; the giant generators for the Psychotron were housed in the lab itself.

Directly in back of the surface generators and completely underground was the ammo dump, the entrance guarded by three Russian soldiers.

Hearing the faint strains of *Ghost Riders in the Sky*, Kagorin frowned in annoyance and turned to the source of the sound, the domed top of the airshaft that led sixty feet below ground to the Psychotron Station and to the living quarters of Dr. Popvikin and his staff.

Kagorin wished that he could slowly strangle Dr. Popvikin —with piano wire! The stupid Ukrainian pig-slop! Him and his American music! And he always played it so loud! Why, Moscow even furnished him LP records by American music groups in an effort to keep him happy and contented. This latest record, this *Ghost Riders in the Sky*, was the most ridiculous of all! Imagine! Apparitions galloping through the sky on stallions! Typical bourgoisie fantasy! Well, everyone knew that Americans were not right in the head.

On the other side of the compound were the storerooms, the mess hall, and the garage, the latter containing spare parts for the T-54 tanks. Most important of all, because the base was supposed to be a weather station, was the meteorological building, one hundred feet west of the storerooms.

So innocent and innocuous the place looked—perhaps because it actually was a meteorological station, staffed by two Russian meteorologists who did collect weather data. Odd birds they were too . . . always talking about isotherms, temperature gradients, magnitudes of irregular fluctuations, etc.

Kagorin looked upward. There, rising from the roof of the weather station, was the electrical recording wind vane and the deflection anemometer.

He smiled in pride and assurance. For now, this base was his Kremlin, his "fortress." Such intricate and detailed planning had gone into the construction of the base. For instance the weather station building was one of the most important features of the above-ground complex. For next to its short, four-legged wind-vane tower was an opening which, when the cover slid back, permitted the passage of the Psychotron wave-antenna—telescoping sections of barium-coated steel that, when raised from the underground lab, projected up through the west wall and on through the roof, to rise seventy-four feet, at maximum, when the Psychotron was in operation.

Itself a masterpiece of hidden construction, the underground Psychotron complex (and living quarters of Dr. Popvikin and his staff) could be reached via two sets of steps, spiraling stairs in tubes, one of which led down from the radio shack connected to the weather station. The second set of stairs led from the back of the lab up to a corner of one of the Russian barracks. To transfer supplies and equipment up and down, there was a freight elevator, the above-ground opening in the north end of the garage.

Kagorin surveyed the desert outside the compound. Nothing but sand and rock and emptiness . . . nothingness in the middle of more nothingness. He sniffed the air—hot, dry . . . and the faint odor of onion soup drifting from the mess hall.

He saw Colonel Andrei Vertesbiesk, who was in charge of the Russian soldiers and who had just come out of the mess hall, walking toward him.

109

In his fifties, lean, trim and brutish looking, Vertesbiesk had seen action in World War II and had been awarded the Order of Stalin for bravery at Stalingrad.

"You're sure they will come?" Vertesbiesk asked, picking at his tobacco-stained teeth.

"Camellion and the Israelis know we're here and have no choice but to try to destroy us," Kagorin replied. "If our positions were reversed, we'd have to do the same."

"There's always the possibility that they haven't found the base."

Colonel Kagorin regarded Vertesbiesk with a sad smile—the poor fool! "You can be positive that Assad revealed the location! Why do you think Israeli planes have been so numerous overhead the past few days? Photo reconnaissance, that's why. Do you think that"—and he pointed upward with a jerk of his thumb—"will fool high resolution cameras? No, Colonel, it will not. The Israelis will attack. When all is darkness, they will attack, and Richard Camellion will be leading them."

Colonel Vertesbiesk glanced up at the camouflage covering the entire area, the overhead net, some twenty-four feet above the ground, the top side painted to resemble sand and rocks. But Vertesbiesk realized that such faked topography couldn't fool photograph-interpretation experts—not for long. Yes, the GRU colonel was right: the Israeli Commandos would attack.

As if reading Vertesbiesk's mind, Kagorin asked, "How do you have the tanks deployed?"

He is worried! This is the tenth time I've told him—but Vertesbiesk said, "All ten of them . . . ringing the base . . . two hundred yards outside the perimeter."

Vertesbiesk himself was not the least bit concerned, confident that he had done all he could to protect the valuable Psychotron base, unless the attack came from an entire army. But a commando force? Ridiculous!

Nine anti-aircraft guns were placed strategically around the perimeter of the compound. Let the Israeli planes come! And to the front of the dispensary was a battery of S-77 missiles, mounted on the long, flat bed of a trailer . . . twenty deadly disciples of death . . . their sharpened noses pointing skyward. Another battery of S-77s waited close to the garage. Let the Israeli planes attack!

"Colonel Kagorin, I assure you, the Israelis will not get

through," Vertesbiesk said smugly. "And even if some of them do, they can't possibly get to the Psychotron. It's not only unthinkable, but impossible!"

It had damn well better be impossible Kagorin thought, remembering the message he had received from the Center in Moscow only a few days before, in response to his detailed report that the Bir El Tamadeh experiment had been a success, that Dr. Popvikin had succeeded in increasing the range of the Psychotron to almost 194 miles, and that in a month or more Dr. Popvikin would be ready for the final test, the hypnotic-telepathic experiment. The wave-beam would be directed at another site in the Sinai, to a village of Dr. Popvikin's choosing, and the villagers directed to commit suicide.

Kagorin had given Moscow the bad news also, reporting that Richard Camellion, the man known as the Death Merchant, had kidnaped Hasan El Assad and had undoubtedly forced him to reveal the location of Station 4-FD.

Alexis concluded the report with his observation that Camellion and Israeli commandos would undoubtedly attack the base.

Kagorin had paled when he read the reply from Center. General Semichastny bluntly informed him that he had made one fine mess of not protecting Egypt's Minister of the Interior! Worse, Kagorin was also responsible for letting the Death Merchant kill three valuable SMERSH agents!

The GRU Center had more startling news for Colonel Alexis Kagorin: since Dr. Popvikin had increased the range of the Psychotron, Moscow would choose the city to be annihilated, *and the target was Tel-Aviv!* General Semichastny also made it clear that he was charging Kagorin with the full responsibility for the test being conducted without any interference. The GRU Otdel Director's implication was obvious: if the test didn't come off as scheduled, Kagorin would be recalled to Moscow to answer in person. Kagorin knew what that meant—demotion and transfer, or worse.

Victor Gulyaiev, after reading Moscow's orders, had said, "If the Death Merchant and the Jews interfere with the final experiment, we've had it!"

"Don't you think I know that?" Kagorin snarled.

"What are you going to do?" Victor was worried, knowing that if Kagorin fell from grace, one Victor Gulyaiev would also be viewed by Moscow with a jaundiced eye.

111

"The telepathic test is scheduled three days from now, at eleven at night," Alexis said. "You and I and Merkulov will fly to the base to personally supervise the security and to make sure everything goes as planned. That's all we can do."

Gulyaiev thought for a moment. "Why at night?" he inquired. "Since we're convinced that Camellion will attack during the night, why don't we have Popvikin conduct the test during the daylight hours?"

Kagorin spread his hands in a gesture of helplessness. "I've thought of that, but it seems that sunlight interferes with the Psychotron's effectiveness. Popvikin says it has something to do with ultra-violet light affecting wave motion. You know that he has the final word regarding the device. We're only Security, remember?"

Victor remembered. He also remembered what had happened to other GRU agents who had botched assignments. They had simply vanished . . .

Kagorin wiped his pillar-like neck with a handkerchief, his eyes still sweeping the compound. "Your men are positioned?" he asked Colonel Vertesbiesk.

"In place and waiting," Vertesbiesk replied. "I've got the Egyptians spread out in the mess hall, under the command of Lieut. Minskorski. When the attack comes, I want those excuses for soldiers out of the way—and I've got five men downstairs."

Alexis nodded. *Five soldiers and twelve agents, including Victor, Merkulov, and myself, should be adequate to protect Popvikin and his staff.*

"And I've got ten men at the radio shack entrance and ten more at the garage entrance," Vertesbiesk said. "The freight elevator's been disconnected. I tell you, Colonel, the Commandos will never get through."

Not bothering to reply, Kagorin stared toward the darkening west. The desert was quiet . . . desolate . . . as empty as the head of an Egyptian soldier. There was no breeze.

He walked slowly to the radio shack, determined that if Richard Camellion did attack, it would be the last assault the Death Merchant ever made!

If the final test fails . . . if I have to die . . . I'm taking Camellion to hell with me.

CHAPTER XI

Situated at the northern end of the Gulf of Suez, on the west central coast of the Sinai peninsula, Ayun Mussa is of no real importance to the world. As far as the general run of humanity is concerned, the little town's existence is almost completely unknown. It is just another Arab settlement —but not to the Israelis and the Egyptians. To both Jew and Arab, Ayun Mussa is of more than momentary interest —of concern to the Israelis because it is only twenty-seven kilometers southeast of the lower end of the Suez Canal, is a coastal town and is built around a paved road (Number 55 on Israeli Army maps); of interest to the Egyptians and, consequently, to the Russians, because it not only is close to the canal, but is also a part of the Sinai, the entire peninsula of which the Egyptians consider territory that belongs to them.

Ayun Mussa is not a model for picture post cards. Its harbor is filled with old dhows and motor-powered vessels of vintage make. The sun-hardened brick dwellings, the majority of which are lined up along both sides of the town's lone, long street, are whitewashed and lopsided. There is a single exception, the Quonset hut type structure at the north end of the long street. Painted a pale green, this building is the headquarters of the Israeli Army unit in the area.

Other than a few dingy shops, there isn't much to see in Ayun Mussa, although Western visitors are sometimes fascinated by the sight of black-garbed *Badawi* women, with thick veils hanging over their faces, walking through the center of town.

On this August night, the tiny settlement was also of interest to Richard Camellion. Dressed in jungle-camouflaged fatigues, he was waiting for the final hour of departure, zero-hour, when he and the Israeli commando force would fly the short distance to the Russian Psychotron base. The attack force had been assembled a half mile from the northern edge of town, the area surrounded by Israeli soldiers, whose task it was to keep curious *Badawi* tribesmen away.

Standing in front of the Operations Tent with Israela and Jock, the Death Merchant mentally checked last minute preparations. The three French Frelon helicopters were ready for take off, the first to be used as a decoy, flying five minutes ahead of the second copter that would actually carry the attacking force. The third copter, after a seven-minute interval, would follow the second and land a quarter of a mile behind the commandos.

Knowing that Camellion was weighing the odds of failure against the sweet taste of success, Israela remarked, "The Bedouins have a strong belief in magic . . . you know, good and bad demons, desert spirits and the like. Do you think we should take one or two along for good luck?" Gaily she laughed. "Or try to conjure up a genie like Aladdin did?"

Jock chuckled. "Which do you mean we should take—the Bedouins or the demons?"

We do have a kind of magic Camellion thought. *The magic of modern science!* There was the special equipment that Gordon Norstead had requested from the CIA and that had been flown in from the United States only a few days before, devices without which the attack would be truly suicidal. For example, the PPS-14 "foliage penetration" surveillance radar. Originally developed by U.S. Army engineers at the Army's Land Welfare Laboratory at Aberdeen, Maryland, for spotting the enemy at night in the thick, black jungles of Viet Nam, the amazing device was capable of amplifying light 40,000 times, making it possible for one to literally "see" in the dark.

The Israelis had tested PPS-14-FP in the desert outside the Beer Sheba Israeli Air Force base. The device had worked perfectly. In pitch blackness, tanks had been outlined in stark, eerie clarity!

The commandos had been divided into two squads of ten men each. Each squad had been equipped with three PPS-14-FPs, while Camellion, Jock, and two commandos of Jock's squad carried what was known simply as *The Box*. About the size of a cigar box and weighing less than ten pounds, it was a radar penetration apparatus capable of seeing underground, to a depth of twenty-three feet and through brick and cement walls. *The Box* was also a product of the United States' Land Warfare lab at Aberdeen.

Camellion smiled, one that was almost malicious. "We've got a kind of 'magic,' " he said, "a sort of 'magic' that makes

114

Aladdin look like an amateur. He only rubbed a lantern, and all he could do was make a genie appear. But modern technology has made it possible for us to merely push a button and make humanity disappear. Of course, Aladdin's genie didn't have atomic weapons . . ."

"If we can make that bloody Mind Blaster disappear, I'll be satisfied," Jock said, hooking his thumbs into the belt that supported the .45 Colt on his hip. "Doubly so if we get back alive. Come to think of it, that's the only thing that worries me about being dead—I don't know a damn thing about it!"

"What you've just said is only another example of mankind's talent for nonsense," Camellion said. He glanced at his wristwatch—10:17. "We spend our lives acquiring knowledge for the purpose of gaining conscious control over the events of existence; then, when the most important of all such events occurs, we haven't the faintest idea of what to expect!"

Israela, who was a very devout Jew, couldn't resist saying, "I thought you didn't believe in a life after death, Richard?"

"I don't, in spite of what the imperialists of righteousness say. Actually, what fascinates me is the thought of oblivion!"

The talk of death bothering Jock, he changed the subject, saying that they were as ready as they'd ever be. "All we have to do now is wait, synchronize our take-off with the attack planes from Beer Sheba, and then go in and blow hell out of the Psychotron base."

Looking out toward the three helicopters, to where the twenty commandos were waiting, squatting on the ground around Coleman gas lanterns, smoking and talking, he concluded with pride, "We 'ave the best fighting men in the world. They'll make short work of that bloody Ivan base."

One of the commandos detached himself from the group and strode over to the Operations Tent. A young man, not yet thirty, blond, tall and radiating good health, Captain Hayim Dafna glanced at the Death Merchant, then—out of respect for Jock who was officially in command—said, "Sir, the force is divided into two squads, with you leading one and I the other. Right?"

"That's what I said at the briefing," Jock replied. "What's the problem?"

"No problem, only I was thinking . . . instead of each

115

squad taking two bazookas, why not take one—a bazooka for each squad? The less we carry, the faster we can move."

Jock glanced searchingly at Camellion, who shook his head. "Each squad will carry two bazookas, Captain Dafna. The Russian military commander at the base will undoubtedly have his T-54s deployed around the perimeter, and I'm not convinced that our planes will be able to knock them out. We'll have to. Keep in mind, too, that the tanks will probably be disguised as sand dunes and what-have-you, but we won't have any trouble spotting them with the PPS-14-FPs or knocking them out."

Captain Dafna was skeptical. "Personally, I don't think the bazookas will do the job, not against a T-54. That model has a very low silhouette and almost four inches of armor plate. We need anti-tank artillery!"

"The bazookas we 'ave will do the job!" Jock interjected. "They're modern versions of the German *Panzerschreck*, or 'Tank Terror.' And don't forget, me boy, each bazooka shell has eight extra ounces of pentolite . . . more than enough explosive to do the job."

"We could blast through ten inches of armor if we had to," Camellion said. "Don't worry about it, Captain. The pentolite will do the job and then some."

Dafna nodded and fumbled in his shirt pocket for cigarettes. He looked squarely at the Death Merchant, on whose smudged face played flickering shadows.

"Then all my squad has to do is get in, blast the surface of the base and hold it while you three hit the underground section?" Dafna said, touching the flame of his lighter to the tip of his cigarette.

"Affirmative," Camellion said. "Kill anything that moves topside and watch out for tanks and half-tracks from Suez —just in case."

Nodding, Captain Dafna adjusted the UZI slung over his shoulder and leisurely rejoined his men.

Camellion's eyes followed him. "Do you think he's afraid?" he asked.

"Of course," Israela said. "He wouldn't be able to do a good job if he weren't."

The tent flap parted and a soldier stepped out, the radio operator who was attached to the Israeli Army platoon stationed at Ayun Mussa.

Stepping up to Jock, the radio operator saluted smartly.

"Sir, Beer Sheba just called," he said. "The bombers and fighters took off four and a half minutes ago."

Camellion glanced at his watch once more. Excellent! Right on schedule! Would their dying be as punctual?

"Very well," Jock said to the man. "Radio back that we're all set here. Keep on the wave length to both Beer Sheba and Tel-Aviv. You have the code book for our messages. That's all."

"Yes, sir." Saluting once more, the radio operator returned to the short wave set in the tent.

Picking up a bull horn, Jock turned it on and addressed the commandos and the pilots of the helicopters, speaking in Hebrew—"Commandos, board number two plane. Number one craft will take off in exactly 13 minutes!"

Jock put down the bull horn and, watching the men prepare to board the helicopter, wondered if he'd be alive two hours later—or if any of them would. The hell with the Death Merchant and his "oblivion!"

Richard Camellion looked up at the moonless sky, welcoming the vastness and the blackness. Blinking bits of blue ice, the stars stared back at him. Were they laughing?

The same sky, the same vastness and the same stars were twinkling down at Colonel Alexis Kagorin—and Camellion asked himself: *Are they snickering at me or at Kagorin?*

He'd know in an hour.

CHAPTER XII

The attacking Israeli aircraft—two Vatour bombers and three French Mystère fighters—had taken off from the IAF Beer Sheba base and, flying west, had streaked in purposely low to foil radar on the Egyptian side of the Canal. With the road from Suez to the Psychotron base being their first target, they bombed a tiny section of it, destroying their main objective, a fifty-foot bridge that crossed a deep ravine. Then, reaching the Psychotron base, the planes dived in at almost zero altitude, the roar of their jets a howling cyclone of ear-shattering sound. Like avenging angels from some Jewish Apocalypse, the planes went about the business of scattering Death, the two sleek Vatours dropping a dozen or more 500-pound demolition bombs and scores of 25-pound incendiaries of the phosphorous-thermite variety.

Tremendous explosions rocked the area. The mess hall flew into a billion pieces of splintered wood—and so did the Egyptians inside, as well as their comanding officer, Lieut. Minskorsky . . . into bits of shattered bone and chunks of bloodied flesh. They were the lucky ones! The ones who didn't die instantly became victims of phosphorous! Shrieking, they stumbled about in horrible agony while the flesh burned and dripped from their bodies.

One of the Russian barracks vanished in a giant flash of flame. The dispensary and the warehouse building disintegrated into nothingness. Along with their loaders and gunners, a half dozen anti-aircraft guns flew twenty feet into the air, falling back as twisted metal and rag-doll corpses.

A bomb exploded close to the weather station, the concussion caving in the west side of the building. While the wall rushed inward, the roof fell downward, and with the collapse of both, the weather tower toppled over into the crater made by the bomb. With it collapsed the fragile and sensitive Psychotron wave antenna which, preparatory to the telepathic-hypnosis test, had been raised to its maximum height of seventy-four feet. The thin antenna had shaken violently, like a tall silver whip lashed by a tornado. Then, as wall and roof caved in, the steel antenna snapped at that spot where it projected upward from the opening next to the weather tower. Weaving, a long line of twisting silver against the smoke and flames, the antenna collapsed onto the sand . . . seventy-four feet of utter uselessness.

Because the compound presented such a small target against the tremendous speed of the jets, the results were not as good as Major Annenberg, the Flight Commander, had hoped for. He had wanted to demolish every single building on the surface! But perhaps the Mystères would complete the job.

The fighters dived in low, secure against the Russian anti-aircraft guns whose barrels could not depress to fire at such low flying aircraft and swerving to avoid the S-77 missiles streaking up at them. Zooming in, the Mystères dropped their 165-gallon napalm canisters, which burst into rolling seas of pure hell-fire, oceans of intense heat that boiled and spread with all the fury and hatred of a tidal wave of lava.

Instantly the remaining two barracks blossomed into flame, as well as the half demolished weather station building. One napalm canister exploded on the remains of the dispensary, the leaping clouds of seething fire engulfing the crews of four more anti-aircraft guns. Screaming, the jellied gasoline eating at their flesh, the unfortunate Russians became blazing torches, dying within seconds in almost unbelievable agony.

Their task completed, the Israeli planes made a wide, banking turn, gaining altitude for the return flight to Beer Sheba. That's when the remaining S-77 missiles—the ones not destroyed by the bombing and the napalm—zeroed in on them.

One Vatour became a brilliant display of red and orange as an S-77 found its under-belly and exploded, killing the crew instantly. Another deadly S-77 made contact with a Mystère. A bright glimmer of flame! Plane and pilot dissolving into eternity!

A second Mystère came to the end of its destiny. A twinkling flash of bursting red! Then nothing but twisted and broken metal, and bits of flesh falling to the cold sands of the desert.

The other Vatour was more fortunate. Apparently defective, an S-77 exploded prematurely, rocking the aircraft violently and causing it to lose altitude. Yet Major Annenberg managed to regain control, quickly acquiring altitude and heading the bomber through the night for Beer Sheba, the last Mystère trailing after him.

119

Colonel Constantine Alexis Kagorin stared into the TV screen, his fierce eyes glued to the destruction taking place sixty feet above him, his mind gorged on the banquet of hatred he felt for Richard Camellion.

Three of the surface monitoring television cameras had been knocked out, the only one still in operation attached to one corner of the tank maintenance garage—not that it really mattered! Alexis knew that with the destruction of the Psychotron antenna, the most important of all the experiments would never take place. He also knew he would never get another promotion! It would be a miracle if he kept the rank of Colonel . . . General Semichastny? Kagorin thought of how Semichastny had taught him to make enemy agents talk by applying a blow-torch to their armpits! No . . . Semichastny, that sadistic tyrant, wouldn't accept any excuses.

Also clustered around the TV screen were Victor Gulyaiev and N. G. Merkulov. They too experienced a feeling of dread over the loss of the hypnotic-telepathic experiment— and, along with Kagorin, they were thinking about the solution to the same problem: how to explain the failure to The Center.

Almost in tears, Dr. Yuri Popvikin paced back and forth, up and down the length of the eighty-foot long Psychotron lab, half talking to himself and to Dr. Vasili Sergeyev, his chief assistant and the physicist with whom he had formulated the theory of electrodynamic life fields. A tall man with a face that looked as though it had been sculptured, Dr. Sergeyev kept shaking his head and saying, "Tch, tch, tch . . ."

All at once, Popvikin rushed over to Colonel Kagorin, his long legs pumping like over-worked pistons, his lab coat flying out behind him. "DO SOMETHING! STOP THEM!" he screamed in a high voice. "Already they have destroyed my tower! Are you just going to sit there and watch television and wait for them to come down here? Moscow will hear of your inefficiency, Colonel . . . yes they will!!!" He began to scratch his thinning hair, his fingers digging into his scalp like talons.

Dr. Sergeyev added, "The equipment must be protected at all costs! Tch! Tch! It will take months to repair the damage . . . months . . ." His fingers fumbled with the lapels of his white smock and, almost in reverence, the way a mother looks at her first-born, he gazed at the giant computer and at

120

the tremendous L-shaped psychotron itself. He stared at the controls and at the latest piece of complicated equipment that had been perfected within the last few weeks—the Mind-Control Alpha Wave Sensor. Ahh . . . the final touch . . . such a marvelous device, by which minds could be controlled at great distances. By wearing the Sensor Control-Helmet the operator could transmit his thoughts—his commands—into the Sensor and hence to the Psychotron, and finally, via the wave-antenna, into the minds of the "target"—literally thousands of people, their number as well as the area and distance depending on the synchronization of the Psychotron's calibration system; and since the Psychotron's Neuron Neutralizers removed all resistance in the victims' minds, they had no choice but to submit to the will of the operator, even if he ordered murder or suicide.

And this final test would have proved it!

"Moscow will hear about this—this gross neglect of duty!" Popvikin screeched, shaking a bony finger at Colonel Kagorin. "You are permitting those maniacs to destroy my greatest invention! You are—"

"SHUT UP, YOU STUPID SON OF A BITCH!" Kagorin bellowed at him, then motioned angrily to several nearby GRU agents. He spoke sharply, but the feeling of his helplessness deepened. "Take this idiot and every member of his staff to their quarters and keep them there—and don't let any of them come back out here."

Hearing Kagorin's order, Colonel Andrei Vertesbiesk, the Red Army tank specialist, came up to him. "Have you forgotten that the barrack entrance leads down to a passageway directly off the staff's living quarters?" he asked.

"I haven't forgotten anything!" Kagorin snapped. He leaned back in the short-backed chair and looked directly at Vertesbiesk. The rumble of more surface explosions drifted down, and all eyes darted up toward the reinforced ceiling. "We've got soldiers back there," Alexis continued. "They can protect Popvikin if an attack should come from the barrack entrance. The electric eyes will give them plenty of warning —and I'd suggest you join your men, Colonel. We'll handle things out here."

Kagorin turned his head and closed his mouth, his manner indicating that, to him, the matter was settled. He resumed watching and glaring at the television screen.

Colonel Vertesbiesk didn't reply. Turning, he headed toward the living quarters of the underground complex, while N. G. Merkulov, staring at the ceiling, said, "What happens to us down here if the ammunition bunker blows?" He looked at Kagorin, then at Gulyaiev, who was also absorbed in the top-side destruction. All at once the screen went blank, the last monitoring camera apparently having been reached by the all consuming flames.

Built like a boxer, Merkulov, this double agent who had posed as "John Cecil Evers," was a handsome man, but it was the way he moved and spoke that gave him personality. He had quick movements and perfect coordination, and didn't believe in anything except loyalty to the Communist Party and to the GRU Otdel.

From out of the corner of his eye, Victor Gulyaiev looked at Kagorin, wondering how soon the GRU chief would make final strategy plans, but knowing better than to ask him. To break the strained silence, Victor said to Merkulov, "The ammo bunker is reinforced with solid steel plating, and the ceiling is ten feet thick and also reinforced. Isn't that right, Alexis?"

Kagorin did not bother to answer. His attention had become centered on an odd looking weapon that resembled an automatic pistol, lying on one of the work tables. Another of Popvikin's toys! A laser pistol he called it! The addle-headed, moronic *kolkhozniki!* Wasting his time on such irrational pursuits. Perhaps if he hadn't fooled around with such nonsense, if he had devoted his full time to the Psychotron, then maybe the final experiment could have been conducted days ago . . . even weeks ago! Damn Popvikin to the deepest part of hell!

Hating the scientist, Alexis got up, went quickly to the bench, picked up the laser pistol and inspected it. The butt was solid wood, and the barrel—if it could be called that—was nothing more than a pencil-thin tube, in the end of which was a very tiny hole, no more than a sixth of an inch in diameter. Where the shell extractor opening of an ordinary pistol was located, this weapon had only a smooth unbroken surface, except for a half inch square toward the back, close to where the rear sights should have been. Hmmmm . . . perhaps a reloading chamber. In the vicinity where some automatic pistols have a hammer was a small button. Trigger in the conventional position. But no trigger guard.

Kagorin pointed the laser gun at the steel door that led to

122

the small passageway outside the lab, containing the stairs that led up to what had been the radio communications center.

He pulled the trigger. Nothing happened. He pressed the button in the end of the weapon and again pulled the trigger. There was no sound, not even the faintest of vibrations as a thin white beam of light—appearing solid in its brilliance—shot from the gun to the door. Almost miraculously a hole appeared in the inch-thick steel! With an evil, calculating smile, Kagorin looked at the gun. Well now, this "toy" did have distinct possibilities.

Still smiling, he put the gun back on safety and tucked the odd-looking weapon in his belt. A plan forming in his mind, he looked slowly around the large Psychotron lab. To one side of the steel door that led to the stairs was the computer. Across the front of the lab, and covering the length of the south wall, was the L-shaped Psychotron. Toward the back of the lab, to the other side of the steel door, was the electrical generator, and across from it the electrical booster, its 9-foot balance wheel spinning furiously at 3,700 RPM.

Alexis Kagorin shook with hatred. *If a tank shell doesn't kill that bastard Camellion, I certainly will!*

He swung around to Merkulov and Gulyaiev, an insane look of fury clouding his face. "Here's what we're going to do," the GRU colonel said . . .

Lying on his belly, propped up on his elbows and staring at the burning base through a pair of binoculars, the Death Merchant felt that he and the commandos had two enemies —the Russians up ahead and the desert, this God-forgotten area of scarred and lacerated earth . . . stricken sterile by the sun and bleach-whipped by the cutting wind . . . stubbed with protruding basalt rock, covered by bone-dry brush and patrolled by venomous yellow scorpions. One hour after dawn the temperature was usually 100! The nights were always cold. But now, Camellion wasn't even chilly, nor were the others. To the contrary, they were soaked with the sweat of tension and apprehension.

Lying next to him, Israela whispered, "The fires are dying down. We'll be able to move in soon."

Without replying, Camellion continued to stare through the binoculars. The burning base illuminated the area, tossing off fantastic shadows that danced and weaved across the desert; yet the glow was still too weak to permit the Russians in the tanks to see the Israelis scattered and lying in the sand . . . waiting . . .

The T-54 tanks also waited, outlined darkly against the brightness of the flames.

"You know, it's possible that they don't know we're here!" Jock said to Camellion.

"They're hoping we'll come to them," Israela said, thinking of the past hour. Everything had gone well. As it flew across the canal, the decoy copter had been hit several times by small arms fire from the ground, without any serious damage being done. Carrying the commandos, the second helicopter had also escaped damage, and so had the stand-by Frelon.

The landings had been made on schedule, just as the attacking IAF planes were banking for the return trip to Beer Sheba. With a sick feeling from watching the bomber and the two fighters shot down, the two commando squads had taken positions around the demolished Psychotron base, keeping back to a distance of at least one thousand yards. Cautiously, Captain Dafna and his squad began working their way to the opposite side of the base, Jock and Camellion having decided that a two-pronged attack would hasten the success of the highly dangerous mission.

"Jock, get on the walkie-talkie and give the order to attack," Camellion said. "By the time we get past the tanks, the fires will have subsided and we'll be able to work on the underground installations!"

"If there is an underground complex!" Israela said.

"There has to be," Camellion replied. "The Ivans wouldn't risk exposing such an important invention above ground, where it would be open to bombing."

No sooner had Jock given the order to fire than the bazooka teams of Captain Dafna opened up on the opposite side of the compound, catching the Russian T-54s completely by surprise. The bazooka boys didn't even have to use the PPS-14 device—not yet, as the tanks could still be seen by the light of the burning base.

A bazooka team would aim, fire, and then move quickly to a new location, a method that quickly blew apart three Soviet tanks. Against the bazooka shells, super-charged with extra pentolite, the T-54s didn't have a chance.

Then Jock's squad went into action, the two bazooka teams moving up and sighting in on the Russian tanks that now had begun lumbering out toward them, the Ivans apparently having decided to carry the battle to the Israelis.

WHOOOMMMMMM! A bazooka shell caught a T-54 directly below its turret, killing the Commander, the gunner and the loader and causing the tank to burst into flames. Immediately, the driver tried to escape through the forward hatch. He was cut to pieces by UZI and FN rifle fire the moment he stuck his helmeted head through the opening. Then the fire reached the tank's ammunition and the T-54 blew itself apart.

Russian soldiers, escaping the bombing and the napalm because they had been outside the perimeter of the base, began moving out into the desert, using the T-54s for protection, some of the Ivans trying to sight in on the Israelis with infra-red rifle scopes.

Another T-54 exploded, but this time the bazooka team that had torn the tank into thirty-two tons of twisted metal also died, from the slugs of another tank whose Commander, having opened the hatch to the cupola, was furiously firing the turret's 7.64 machine gun. A commando took aim with an FN rifle, pulled the trigger, and the Russian commander dropped back down into the tank, feeling stupid over being dead.

Camellion and his two companions then saw it—the T-54 moving toward the rise on which they were lying. They squirmed back quickly to the bottom of the miniature hill and, keeping low, ran to another position, machine gun slugs snapping at the sand and rock above them.

They paused, forty yards away, to the left side of the Russian tank, just as the monster sent a shell to their former position. Clicking on the walkie-talkie, Jock contacted Captain Dafna. The news was grim. While five T-54s had been destroyed on the opposite side of the compound, Dafna had lost four men and had also been wounded in the shoulder by shrapnel from a Russian hand grenade. Then, contacting Sgt. Bloom, Jock got the bad news about his own squad. One man dead and another gut-shot!

Even as Jock clicked off the walkie-talkie, two more commandos of his squad lost all their luck in life. They didn't even have time to scream as a T-54's 100MM cannon boomed, blowing them into the next world.

In the darkness, the Death Merchant's face became grim. "This can't go on," he said calmly. "We're losing men, and we're still not an inch closer to the base!"

"What do you suggest?" asked Jock, his voice heavy with tension.

"The tank approaching the rise!" Richard said. "I'm going to capture it."

His eyes seemed to stab holes in the darkness as he searched the smudged, taut faces of Jock and Israela. "Can either of you drive a T-54?"

"I can," Jock replied, thinking of the difference between keeping your chin up and sticking your neck out, "but how do you think that—"

"Come on, we'll follow this gully," Richard said. "If we can get in the proper position, we'll be in business."

With Camellion in the lead, they crept along in the darkness, moving in what was nothing more than a wide, sloping ditch, until at last the Death Merchant judged they were in the strategic position, the one they needed to have the advantage.

They crawled up the sandy mound, Camellion taking "The Box" from the kit-bag slung over his shoulder. He switched on "The Box" and pointed a probe at the area directly ahead. There it was—the T-54 that had fired on them, outlined on the radar screen . . . not more than thirty feet in front of them. Behind the tank were a dozen or more Russian soldiers.

Israela threw the safety off her UZI. "So how do we do it?" she whispered.

Removing the kit bag, Richard placed it on the sand and returned "The Box" to its special compartment. He took out several smoke grenades which he clamped to his combat belt. "The two of you handle the Ivans behind the tank," he said. "I'll take care of the joker in the turret. Open fire the moment I'm out in the open. But first, Jock, radio our boys not to open fire on that particular T-54."

Several minutes later, after relaying the order to his squad, Jock said, "I've got an Israel flag we can hang on the aerial as a signal to our men."

"And make us a target for the Ivans!" Israela said, her tone suggesting that she considered the idea ridiculous.

To a certain extent, their eyes had become accustomed to the darkness, and they could see barely the dark bulk of the

Russian tank, which had turned slightly in its path and was clanking in a direction diagonal to them.

Bringing up their UZIs, Jock and Israela glanced up briefly at the Death Merchant, who, having leaped to his feet, was dashing across the open space toward the creaking T-54. Caught off guard by the suddenness of the action, the Russian soldiers attempted to cut down the running, weaving figure, one of them almost succeeding in getting off a shot before Jock and Israela chopped them to pieces with a storm of machine-gun fire.

Standing up in the turret, on the Commander's platform, with his body exposed to the waist, the Russian Commander jerked his head toward the Death Merchant, surprise and alarm freezing him for a moment. Since the machine gun was mounted on the front of the turret, directly in front of the hatch, he couldn't swing the weapon toward the Death Merchant, who was beyond the alti-azimuth angle of the gun; and he certainly didn't have time to work the rotation lever and swing the turret.

The Russian did see the flashes from Jock's and Israela's UZIs as they machine gunned the soldiers following the tank. Apparently thinking that the two concealed commandos were more of a danger than Camellion, he did a very stupid thing: he reared up in the turret and attempted to throw a hand grenade at them, looking enormously astonished when Camellion's slugs ripped open his chest and knocked him against the rim of the hatch-opening. He fell from the turret, going over backwards, the hand grenade falling to the opposite side of the tank and exploding with a roar, killing three soldiers crouched against the side skirts for protection. But even before they had time to fall back to the sand, the Death Merchant was leaping up on the tank and tossing the smoke grenades into the open hatch.

A bullet from a Russian rifle zinged dangerously close, striking one of the turret's handholds and then flying off into space. Another slug tore at the cloth of his left leg. Two more pings, one on either side of him! Richard jumped from the tank, hitting the sand feet first—then getting in close to the side of the T-54, which suddenly ground to a halt, its engine idling . . . and what seemed to be tons of smoke pouring from its turret hatch.

Camellion waited by the side of the tank, hoping the smoke would fill the interior before the gunner or loader had the presence of mind to toss the grenades back through the turret . . . counting on panic to overpower common sense. Panic did precisely that, aided by the desire to survive. The tank crew knew they could either remain in the steel coffin and suffocate or else crawl out and take their chances. Hearing the hand grenade go off and smelling the smoke, they falsely assumed the tank had been hit.

Coughing violently, gasping and choking, a Russian began crawling from the turret. Half blinded by smoke, he did not see the Death Merchant waiting by the side of the tank.

Directly behind the tank's front glacis plate was the forward hatch—to the left side—which now was flung open, as the driver began pulling himself out amidst a cloud of smoke that also rushed out of the hatch. The third Ivan crawled over the side of the turret, clawing his way out to fresh air.

A few seconds later, the Death Merchant opened fire with his UZI, and the three tankmen began clawing their way into hell.

Jock and Israela darted down the incline and Jock pulled a half-sized Israel flag from the breast pocket of his fatigues. Israela handed Richard his bag, and he took from it a gas mask which he slipped over his head.

"We don't have time to wait until the smoke dissipates," Camellion said. "The other tanks will try to blast us, and the sooner we get this one moving, the better off we'll be." He took the flag from Jock and unfurled it.

Putting on their gas masks, Jock and Israela nodded.

Shortly—after Camellion had attached the flag to the turret's five foot radio aerial—the three commandos were inside the Russian tank, Israela standing on the turret turntable and Jock in the forward driver's seat, his hands on the track steering controls, his feet resting lightly on the brake and gear shift controls. From his reclined position, he attempted to see the outside through the driver's periscope. Impossible! The smoke was still too thick. Jock raised the driver's seat to a fully upright position. There. That was better. Now he could see through the opening of the hatch.

The Death Merchant stood on the Commander's turret control platform, hunched down and firing the machine gun attached to the outside forward rim of the turret, his stream of slugs knocking over other Russians clustered around the back of another tank, about sixty feet away.

Israela had found the two smoke grenades, still spewing

128

smoke and had thrown them out the main hatch. Gradually the smoke began to clear from the interior.

Camellion dropped back down into the tank. "Jock, call our boys and let them know that we have this tank and are going to take it straight in to the base," he said. "Tell them to watch for the flag on the aerial."

Jock began talking on the walkie-talkie while Camellion and Israela fanned out the remaining smoke. Jock switched off the walkie-talkie, reversed the driver's seat to its reclining position, then peered into the periscope. Ah, much better. He could see clearly. Uh huh . . . Russian soldiers creeping up on the tank. Well, the Ivans didn't have a bazooka, but suppose they carried high-powered plastic explosive? Why the bloody blokes might blow a track, or even the entire tank!

"SLAM YOUR HATCH, CAMELLION!" Jock called out. "COMPANY'S COMING—HANG ON!"

Jock closed the driver's hatch. Then, throwing the mobile fortress into gear, he disengaged one track and skidded the other, turning the tank completely around. Pointing the tank in the direction of the Psychotron base, he gave the T-54 more gas, and it crawled across the desert at an amazing 18 miles per hour, its 600 HP engine roaring. The T-54 could do 32 MPH, but only on a smooth surface.

Vaguely wishing that he had brought along a thermos of iced V-8 vegetable juice, the Death Merchant, now sitting in the gunner's seat, familiarized himself with the controls of the 100MM turret gun, the main armament of the tank, noting with satisfaction that the weapon was controlled by the very latest of equipment. *I should be! The Ivans copied everything from the Americans and the Germans!*

Not bad! The Range Finder was of the Stereoscopic type, with—yes, there they were—built-in autocollimators to eliminate the need for time-consuming calibration; there was also a ballistic computer which made sighting practically automatic. Fine! Range Finder computer and sighting periscope were connected by electronic servos so that the 100MM gun was aimed, locked into position and ready for firing as soon as ranging was completed.

Without warning, the T-54 lurched, almost throwing Richard and Israela to the turret turntable floor—and Jock yelled up at them, "YOU'D BETTER GET THAT GUN IN OPERATION, CAMELLION. AN IVAN TANK 'AS

129

SPOTTED OUR FLAG AND IS TRYING TO RANGE IN ON US!"

Again he skidded one track, almost spinning the tank and cutting a new path, a course that headed the tank for the base at a right angle.

"Put a shell in the breech," Camellion ordered Israela. He tested the power traverse and elevation controls, first swinging the turret, then raising and lowering the 100MM gun. Everything was in perfect order.

Grateful that she had received intense tank training in the Israel Army, Israela inspected the projectile storage area on the floor of the turret turntable.

"Explosive or armor piercing," she said. "Take your choice, lover!"

"Armor piercing," he replied.

Israela lifted a 40-lb. projectile and shoved it into the open breech. Next came the bagged charge, which she rammed in behind the shell. She then closed and locked the breech.

The Death Merchant tore off his gas mask and stared into the gunner's periscope, one hand pulled the traverse control lever as he moved the turret and searched for an enemy tank. Ah ha! There!—in the 'scope's cross-hairs, the armored-plated sideskirts of a T-54. But only for a moment! The enemy tank turned at an angle, and Camellion swung his turret to find it. Nothing! A few seconds passed. Once more the T-54 moved across the hair-lines of the scope. Very rapidly he turned the ranging knob and worked the slide for the line-angle of sight elevation, knowing he wouldn't have time to use the small ranging gun to determine whether the main 100MM gun was on target. He judged the distance of the tank to be about seventy yards. He heard it—the buzz as the range finder computer locked—and pressed the firing button. The 100MM cannon roared, shaking the tank, the fume extractor on the long barrel smoking furiously.

The shell caught the enemy tank in the rear of its turret, sending turret and crew in all directions—black smoke and flames pouring from the interior. The driver tried to pull himself through the forward hatch and finally made it; he was sliding down the tank's front glacis plate when a commando cut him in two with a burst of UZI fire. Almost in two separate parts, his body dropped to the sand.

"We got him!" Camellion said to Israela, who had already loaded the 100MM with another shell and bagged charge.

Again the Death Merchant revolved the turret, seeking another T-54—and found one, about a hundred yards or so to the right. Oh damn! Before he could sight in, an Israeli bazooka team from Jock's squad blew it apart!

Camellion continued his searching.

Moving in a direction opposite to the enemy tanks, the now Israeli T-54 was some one hundred yards to the rear of the Russians, between the tanks and the Psychotron base, a position that necessitated Camellion's reversing the turret completely, if he were to find the remaining tanks to his rear.

Very slowly the turret moved. Finally the periscope found the back glacis plate of a T-54—but only briefly! Abruptly, the enemy tank turned, reversing itself so that the muzzle of its 100MM was—for a moment—centered on the Israeli tank.

"Jock—to the left! To the left—dodge!" Camellion yelled, and instantly felt the momentum when Jock broke one track and speeded up the other.

WHHHHOOOOOMMMMMmmmmmmmmm! Barely missing them, the enemy shell exploded with a tremendous concussion, an earth-shaking reverberation that pounded their eardrums, the raining shrapnel a hail storm stabbing the hull.

Camellion, moving the turret slightly, sighted in, fired, and missed . . . his shell exploding five or six yards short.

"ZIG-ZAG IT, JOCK!" the Death Merchant shouted— then, to Israela, "Give me high explosive rounds. I can barely make out some of the Ivans on foot, and I'm going to put those Bolshivik boobs out of action. Load up."

Three times Israela shoved high explosive projectiles and bagged charges into the breech, and three times the DM aimed and fired, each time sending bodies tumbling into the air. Twice more he fired at the other Ruskie T-54 which, apparently, was the only enemy tank remaining on this side of the base area. And each time he missed! Three times the Russian tank fired back, missing each time—due to Jock's uncanny ability to dodge the shells.

Then Jock called out, "We're home, in the compound! I don't see a single Ivan!"

The tracks of the Israeli tank ground heavily into the rubble of the area where the dispensary had stood. Jock brought the tank to a complete stop, twenty feet from the demolished weather station whose fire had burned down to merely smoldering ashes.

That's when the remaining Russian tank—two-hundred yards away—got half-lucky, even if its gunner did miscalculate.

The exploding shell rocked the Israeli tank so violently that Camellion was thrown from the gunner's seat, and Israela to the steel bottom of the turntable.

"I think we've had it!" Camellion said matter of factly.

In desperation, Jock tried to turn the tank, but succeeded only in spinning it in a large circle. The shell had hit the rear of the tank, coming in at an angle, close to the right track's driving sprocket, wrecking the track, throwing it from the last three wheels and shattering the sprocket. Helplessly the tank spun.

Fulmite fumes from the exploded shell began seeping into the stuffy confines of the turret. The bloody bastards! Jock shut off the engine and threw open the hatch above his head. "Come on!" he yelled, "We've got to get the hell out!"

Getting to his feet, Camellion flung back the hatch in the Commander's cupola, but shook his head "NO" at Israela when she glanced up at the opening, through which one could see the black night and the blue stars. "Not up that way," he said. "We'll go through the driver's hatch. That way we'll have the turret between us and the Ivans out there on foot. MOVE!—before that tank can correct its aim and zero in on us."

They saw Jock climbing out the forward hatch as they wriggled through the opening that led to the driver's compartment; soon they too were crawling out the forward hatch, Israela going first and Camellion following. Sliding to the ground, they followed Jock, the three of them taking a position some twenty yards from the wrecked tank, to one side of the base's ammo bunker, whose concrete wall topped with a flat roof rose five and a half feet above the surface of the ground. Jock was talking to Captain Dafna on the walkie talkie.

Shoving Israela down beside Jock, Richard looked out across the windy desert, expecting the Russian tank to throw another round at them. There was a tremendous explosion, a gigantic burst of red and yellow, but it was the remaining enemy T-54 that had blown up. Jock's bazooka team had caught the T-54 in its side, directly below its turret, the bazooka shell exploding in the projectile storage area. The exploding ammo literally blew the tank apart!

132

Jock, switching off the walkie-talkie, turned slowly to Camellion and Israela, the shadows playing over his darkened face. "I told Hayim where we are," he explained. "He and his squad—what's left of them—are coming in."

"And our squad?" Israela asked. Carefully she checked her UZI, then felt in her kit bag to make sure spare clips and fragmentation grenades were readily accessible.

Once more Jock switched on the walkie-talkie. "I'm calling Sgt. Bloom now," he said. "I think all the tanks are destroyed, but how many Ivans are still on foot out there?"

"You'd better tell Bloom to be extra cautious," Richard advised. "If any Ivans are left out there, they'll be dug in and waiting, now that the tanks are kaput."

He and Israela both threw up their UZIs then, watched darkened figures—who dodged first to one pile of debris, then to another—coming toward them, two of the men helping a third who limped. Shortly, Captain Dafna and three other commandos had flattened themselves against the wall of the ammo bunker. There was a bloody bandage around Dafna's head. Another commando had been shot in the leg.

"Is this all that's left of the squad?" Jock asked in a low voice.

"Yes, sir. Six dead, four alive and the objective reached!" Hayim Dafna said, his tone implying that any means justified the end . . . that the dead were worth the goal—and they had to admit, each in his own private thoughts, that he was right.

A series of shots rang out in the desert—Ruskie rifles and machine pistols! Then the snarl of Israeli UZIs. The same thought dominated all of them: who had died—Jews or Slavs?

The walkie-talkie buzzed. Switching it on, Jock held the set to his ear and spoke into the mouthpiece. "Go ahead!" He listened, grinned, replied, "Affirmative—and out!" He clicked off the set. "That was Bloom. He and his squad 'ave finished off the last of the Ivans and are coming in." He glanced at Hayim who had opened a PPS-14-FP and was peering through the darkness, around one corner of the wall, with the binocular radar-scope, looking at the area where the tank maintenance garage had been. Now there was nothing but a concrete block shell.

"More Ivans over there," Dafna said soberly, "about twenty of them behind the walls of that burned-out building. I'm thinking we can make a pincer movement and sneak up and lob in grenades."

"They'll keep us pinned down here until we finish them," another commando said, the one who was wounded in the thigh. He bent down and tightened his bandage.

Swinging his kit-bag around in front of him, Camellion momentarily studied the T-54 he had captured and which now stood disabled, its right track hanging crookedly from the wheel lugs, like a twisted ribbon of heavy flat metal.

"Why not use the tank to blast those Russians out of there?" suggested Camellion, motioning to the tank with a jerk of his thumb. He took "The Box" from the shoulder bag. "You can't move the T-54, but the traverse controls still function and so does the gun elevation system." He pushed back the cover of "The Box's" radar scope and pulled out the foot-long bottom probe, following this by extending the front probe which was directly in front of The Box's oval screen.

"Camellion's got a bloody good idea," Jock said to Captain Dafna. "Hayim, you and George slip over to that T-54 and blast the Ivans hiding out behind those walls. As close as the blighters are, you can blast them at zero degrees inclination."

"Let's go," Dafna said, touching George Immanski, the other commando, lightly on the sleeve. "You aim the gun, George. I'll load."

Crouching, they began dodging toward the wrecked Russian tank, even as other figures approached from the desert and soon were taking up protective positions by the wall—Sgt. Danial Bloom and the remainder of Jock's squad. Only two bazooka men!

"The others are dead," Bloom reported, "except Noah. He got it in the stomach." Bloom motioned toward the darkened desert. "We've made him comfortable out there and can pick him up on the way back. But I doubt if he lives that long."

Grimly, Jock heard a cry in his heart, a moan of loss. Twenty-three commandos, including Jock, Israela and Camellion, had begun the battle. Thirteen were now dead. The loud song of Death dirged loudly in Jock's mind . . . the one chorus in the human symphony that always caused him pain. *A bloomin' paradox, that's what it was. You 'ave to accept Death, but you bloody well hell don't 'ave to like it —or enjoy it like Camellion!*

134

"At last we succeeded in gaining the objective," Jock said to no one in particular, sighing deeply.

"Only halfway!" Richard Camellion said coldly. Taking several steps, he moved to where Jock was standing, and put his hand on Jock's shoulder, his fingers clutching in their urgency. "We're losing time," Richard said. The mask of ice, that personna of insensibility, had dropped from his face, and it had become strangely young. "We've still got to go underground after Colonel Kagorin and his boys. We still have to blow up the Mind Blaster—and Kagorin will be waiting for us."

Jock said nothing. No one else spoke. All that could be heard was the desert wind, the low crackling of the dying fires and the creak of the T-54 turret which was slowly turning, moving the long-barrelled 100MM in the direction of the wrecked garage. Then the long barrel began to lower to zero elevation.

Jock ordered, "Sgt. Bloom, take a few men and try to get closer to the Ivans after Hayim and George slam in a few rounds—and no prisoners. We haven't the manpower to guard them."

The 100MM cannon roared and a large section of the garage wall vanished, concrete instantly changing into dust, and live Russians—flying to all the cardinal points of the compass—into dead ones.

In quick succession, Hayim and George flung four more rounds into the area. Rock flew, walls dissolved, and Russians screamed and died, their broken bodies reddening the sands as far as twenty yards away. Nevertheless, because the garage area was vast, some of the enemy remained alive and began firing toward the tank. Sgt. Bloom and the other commandos returned the fire as they moved in for the wipe-up.

Israela looked at Camellion and saw that the mask had returned to his face. There was no trace of emotion, nothing to betray what he might be feeling or thinking.

The sweet stink of death, of burned debris and barbequed flesh, suddenly made her feel faint, and she moved closer to the Death Merchant, who, holding "The Box" the way a dowser holds a dowsing stick in search of water, began moving across the area, bending low and half-stumbling over wreckage. Progress was slow. The surface of the Psychotron base was a graveyard of devastation, a blackened cake of death and desolation, topped with an uneven frosting of corpses that resembled nothing human . . . that had been partially cremated by napalm and phosporous.

Israela and Jock trailed after the Death Merchant, their UZIs covering the terrain on either side of him. It was evident that Jock felt Camellion was taking a chance on exposing himself—and them. But to Israela it seemed perfectly natural. She realized that those who had gone through experiences that involved playing chess with death never quite lost that particular instinct for self-preservation. Their senses seemed to develop to such a fine edged degree that they saw not only with their eyes but with their backs as well, heard not only with their ears but with their whole bodies, and could judge within a second where the breath of Death was blowing.

Camellion stopped a short distance from the heat-twisted girders of the weather tower. Incredulously, the weather vane and anemometer were still connected to its top! Lying next to the tower, stretching out of the line of vision into the dark desert, was a long snake of steel, the bottom section as thick as a man's thigh. They stared at it, realizing it was some kind of antenna . . . a very unusual kind of antenna.

"Part of the Mind Blaster?" Israela asked in a low voice.

"Whatever it was, it's useless now," Jock said.

The Death Merchant suddenly changed course, still holding "The Box" out in front of him. "According to 'The Box,' there's an opening very close to here," he finally said. He took a few steps . . . paused . . . a few more steps . . . looked once more at the radar-plate of "The Box." He stopped. He looked around the area. Complete carnage stared back, as well as a nearby corpse, the flesh of whose face had been burned away, the skull grinning up at them.

"Right about here," Camellion said, "unless 'The Box' is not working properly." He closed the cover of the radar-scope and returned "The Box" to the bag. Then, kicking at the charred beams—some of which still smoldered—he began clearing the small section, Jock and Israela watching him and the surrounding area. After some minutes, Camellion put on a pair of gloves and began tugging at the rubble, at chunks of concrete, charcoaled timber and fire-burned equipment. He picked up the twisted metal cabinet of a Russian-made short wave receiver and flung it to one side, got to his haunches and stared at what lay at his feet.

136

"There it is," he said, touching the handle with the toe of his combat boot.

Jock and Israela stared at the four-foot square of metal which—after Camellion removed a glove and touched the steel with the tip of his finger—was found to be still warm.

"This has to be one of the entrances," Camellion said. "It's certainly not an airshaft, not with a trap door." He put a fresh clip in his UZI, cocked the machine gun, threw on the safety and continued, "There has to be another entrance and probably an elevator." He faced Jock. "That will be your job, you and the rest of the commandos, to find another entrance and come down from a direction opposite to this one, the one I'm taking."

He grew aware that Israela had reached out and was holding his wrist in a firm grip. "You're—going down there alone?" she exclaimed, dumfounded. "Richard, that's madness! That's—it's suicide!"

Camellion was staring at her, suddenly seeing a young woman of great charm with an air of elegance about her, in spite of her smudged face and combat fatigues. For the first time since he had known her, he took in every detail of her appearance. Even in Egypt, when they had posed as man and wife and lived in the same hotel suite, he had not seen her like this, as a woman. He sensed the questions in her mind, the many unasked questions and answers which lay between them like a deep abyss. Was she wondering why he had not tried to make love to her in Egypt? A terrible desperation rose in him. There was nothing he could ever share with her . . . nothing. His mission in the world could never include love . . . never . . . .

With a quick sure motion, Camellion pulled a Magnum from its hip holster and threw open its cylinder, checking its ammunition and when he answered, it was briskly, with the impersonal, official tone he liked to use in moments of strain or embarrassment. "I'll need room and plenty of it. On those narrow steps, the three of us would only get in each other's way."

"Richard—be careful!" Israela said in a little girl voice.

With a gloved hand, the Death Merchant grasped the large handle of the trap door, then paused and gave her a quick upward glance. "It's the Ivans below on whom the Fates had better smile," he said lightly—then adding in a joking tone,

137

"Personally, I'll have more fun than a part-time sweet potato salesman!"

He glanced at the coiled rope fastened to Jock's gun belt. Convinced that the Psychotron lab itself would be underground, Camellion had insisted that each Commando carry a 50-foot length of braided nylon rope.

"Better give me your rope, Jock," Camellion said. "I might need it, depending on the depth of the passage."

Jock unbuckled the rope and handed it to Camellion, who secured the coil of nylon over his own rope.

Then the Death Merchant pulled up on the trap door.

A square of solid blackness glared back at him.

Colonel Kagorin—I'm coming to kill you!

CHAPTER XIII

After lowering himself into the opening past the trap door, the Death Merchant was surprised to find himself on a metal ladder that led straight down, previous experience in similar situations telling him that he had to be in some sort of anti-chamber to the main stairs. Because of the inconvenience of climbing straight down, it was highly inconceivable that the ladder would lead directly to the Psychotron lab. Cautiously, he climbed down, coming to a platform some ten feet from the mouth of the square opening, his rubber-soled combat boots noiselessly touching the metal surface. He paused in the all-compressing darkness, analyzing the situation. Obviously, Colonel Kagorin had ordered the lights to be turned off in the small passage, no doubt with the faint hope that Camellion would foolishly click on a flashlight and just as stupidly expose himself as a convenient target for waiting GRU agents. Camellion felt insulted. A professional like Kagorin should realize that an old pro wouldn't fall for such a simple trick. To implement his hopes, the GRU boss would probably have agents stationed at the bottom of the main passage, with in-structions not to fire a single shot until positive that Camellion and the Israelis were "dead" in their sights. Yeah—a fine plan! The only flaw was that the Death Merchant had the advantage. He could "see" in the dark! He had "The Box," which he now took from his shoulder bag and put into operation, fastening a facial contour mask to the radar screen in order to view the images without the plate's black-light escaping into the dark-ness and giving away his position.

Just as I suspected! By the soft glow of the screen, Richard deduced that the passageway was a horizontal one, perhaps eight feet long and seven feet high, with the steps that actually led to the Psychotron room located at the opposite end. A careful analysis of the shadowy outlines on the screen further revealed that the stairs spiraled around a center axis con-tained in a tube, whose diameter was almost eleven feet.

But . . . I must be positive! Camellion adjusted the stadio-meter, that part of "The Box" that measured distance.

Right—the diameter was 10 feet 7 inches.

Crawling along on his hands and knees, the Death Merchant felt his way forward, finally coming to the end of the horizontal passage and reaching the edge of the platform from whose center the stairs led downward. Again, Camellion made use of "The Box," carefully reading the stadiometer of the downward probe—49 feet 10 inches. The screen also revealed half a dozen forms clustered within a radius of ten feet of the bottom of the stairs.

They could be watching me with infra-red scopes. But it isn't likely they'll shoot if I crawl out on the platform. They'll wait for others to follow me. And if they do shoot, I'd never know it! I'd be dead—the only game I'll never win.

He crawled out onto the platform and stood erect, "seeing" and picturing his cramped surroundings with his creeping fingers. Then he found the protective pipe railing around the platform.

On the other hand, if they are watching me and I start to go down the stairs and they feel that I'm alone, they might very well blow my head off!

Just to be on the safe side, he turned and made a motion with his hand, as if beckoning to others. *I can't do both! Either I stay up here or go down there. Hmmmmm . . . I wish I had brought along a box of raisins or some figs.*

Standing on his toes, he felt upward, his fingers coming in contact with an I-beam. Further inspection revealed that the axis to which the stairs were mounted was attached to the center of the girder which, in turn, crossed the diameter of the stair-well tube—a simple but effective arrangement.

Going past the stairs to the edge of the platform, he removed the nylon rope he had taken from Jock. Let's see . . . almost fifty feet to the bottom. He cut what he judged to be ten feet from the fifty-foot length of rope, and returned the commando knife to the sheath attached to his back, directly below the nape of his neck. He then climbed onto the railing and, leaning over as far as he could, fastened one end of the forty-foot rope around the girder. *Uh huh, I'll be able to swing out at least six or seven feet from the stairs—and, unless they are watching me, they shouldn't suspect. The end of the rope will be ten feet above them.*

Carefully, he played out the rope until it was dangling down full length; he then returned to the platform and pulled in a section of the rope to tie loosely around the top railing, where he could reach it with convenience. This task completed, he moved back to the out-of-sight security of the horizontal passage, closed "The Box" and returned it to the bag.

Taking his gas mask from the bag, he slipped it on. Next, he took out a smoke bomb and three hand grenades . . . thought for a moment, then removed a pen-light. He checked the UZI and the two .357s in their flap-holsters—and for some ridiculous reason, a poem he had once written loomed in his mind

> *Though the day of my destiny is over,*
> *And the star of my fate has declined,*
> *I'll seek another warm universe*
> *In another continuum of Time . . .*

Camellion put the pen-light on the platform, on the edge closest to him.

But today's not the day to seek another universe!

As though he did this sort of thing every day, he slipped on his gloves, pulled the pins of the hand grenades and dropped them over the edge of the platform . . . one by one . . . knowing that even if the resulting explosions tore the stairs loose at the bottom, the staircase would still not collapse—just in case he needed it later as an escape route. Even if the stairs were blown loose from the top I-beam—which was impossible—they could only wobble about in the tube, like a twelve-inch stick in a twelve-inch bottle.

Covering his ears with his hands, he turned his head, closed his eyes and screamed to equalize the pressure from the explosions—and come they did! ONE! TWO! THREE! Terrific concussions that reverberated within the tube.

The Death Merchant reacted instantly. After tossing down the smoke grenade and clicking on the pen-light, he became a flashing blur of speed as he leaped to the platform, rushed to the railing and untied the rope. Even before the final echo from the explosions had faded away, he was sliding down the forty-foot length of nylon—and not a single second too soon! A veritable hail of machine gun fire leaped up at the point where the pen-light was glowing, some of the slugs ricocheting from the steel platform and stairs and coming dangerously close to the Death Merchant.

With the UZI hanging loosely around his neck, the Death Merchant slid to the end of the rope and dropped to the floor,

141

instantly unsnapping the UZI, which practically flew into his hands. In a crouch, he found himself six or seven feet from the Russian agents who had fired up at what they presumed to be his position on the platform. Someone had turned on a small light at the end of the passage, and Richard could see that the agents were possessed by a furious fit of coughing and that their eyes were streaming from the thick white smoke. Another GRU goof was also gasping. He leaned against the wall opposite to the stairs, his machine pistol hanging loosely in his hand. He glanced up, saw the gas-masked figure and —for only a tiny fraction of eternity—heard the deadly snarl of the UZI. He blinked and died, the red juice of life dribbling from his chest.

The Death Merchant had jumped sideways as he fired. The hot stream of steel from the other two machine pistols flowed harmlessly past him. The two GRU slobs didn't have a single chance, Camellion's own slugs smashing them with a fury that worked a miracle, that instantly knocked them backwards and changed them into corpses.

Through the thick smoke, Camellion saw that besides the three GRU agents he had just killed, four other Ivans lay dead, their mangled bodies evidence that they hadn't been very lucky with the hand grenades, two of the bodies held together only by splintered bones and half-cut tendons.

Silence—except for the whirr of the small ventilating fan, slowly inhaling smoke through the ceiling, and the sound of other machinery . . . the steady chug of electrical motors. The passage was empty, a kind of concrete coffin whose walls were smooth and unbroken. There was one exception, the metal door toward the east end of the passage.

Once more Camellion let "The Box" assist him, the probes and radar-oval revealing that beyond the steel door lay the Psychotron lab. Diligently, the man who dealt in instant death studied the blurred shadows and outlines on the tiny screen. Directly beyond the door was a very large room that contained machinery, not only against the walls but also on the floor. From the sound, Camellion judged some of the machines to be generators of some sort.

Richard studied the pulsations on the screen. There were men scattered about the huge room. It was difficult to tell on the small screen—but at least two or three toward the front and four or five more toward the back. And in back of the group—another wall! He moved "The Box" and adjusted the

142

controls. Another room, in fact, a whole series of small rooms, with a long hallway running down the center of the complex. More figures, a couple of dozen, but the images were not spread out. Camellion decided they must belong to the scientific technicians of the base, placed back there out of harm's way.

That's where I'll find Doctor Popvikin! Kagorin's probably in the lab. All I have to do is go in and get them!

Reaching down and grasping the collar of a dead Russian agent, the Death Merchant dragged the corpse to the far end of the passageway, the end farthest from the steel door. Then, mentally humming a part of Brahms' *Academic Festival Overture,* he returned to the steel door and inspected it. Because of the thickness of the wall, the door was placed in a three-foot offset and he could see that it opened inward. He took two packs of RDX and worked the putty-like explosive around and into the hairline cracks between door and wall. He fastened the ends of the detonating wires to the RDX and, after stringing them out to the end of the passage, connected the ends to a small battery-powered detonator. He turned his back, closed his eyes, opened his mouth and screamed—then clicked the switch.

The terrific explosion filled the passage with a roar that sounded like a T-54 100MM! There was another thunderous crash as the steel door was flung inward, smashing to the floor amid a cloud of smoke and the acrid stink of burnt nitrocellulose.

But no machine gun fire came through the smoking opening!

They want me to come to them! Very well. I shan't disappoint Colonel Kagorin!

With great effort, the Death Merchant picked up the corpse of the Russian he had dragged to the end of the passage and, keeping to the wall and holding the dead GRU agent as a shield, advanced to the blasted doorway. When only a foot away from the door, he managed to remove a hand grenade attached to his belt. Holding the corpse close to him, he flattened himself against the wall, pulled the pin and tossed the grenade through the opening.

WHHHOOMMMMMMMMM!—immediately followed by a sizzling river of machine gun fire, the slugs hitting the wall opposite the door and ricocheting in all directions, one glancing across Camellion's right arm, by the elbow, digging a

143

small blood ditch, another whizzing by his cheek. No time for physical inspection though. Time now only for movement, for speed and surprise!

Still standing to the side of the doorway, Camellion pushed the corpse into the Psychotron lab, shoving the body with all his strength, at an angle that sent the dead man in the direction opposite to the side on which Camellion was standing.

Now—ATTACK! Crouching almost to his knees, his UZI in his moist hands, the Death Merchant flung himself into the Psychotron lab, keeping to one side of the doorway. Since he was still alive and not full of machine gun slugs, Camellion knew his plan had worked. That split second had been enough, that tiny trickle of time in which the corpse had fallen through the doorway. Colonel Kagorin, waiting behind one corner of the electrical Booster, and the others hadn't had the time to distinguish features and clothing, reacting automatically in their hatred and almost dissecting the corpse with machine gun fire. Never was a dead man filled with so much steel!

The Death Merchant, half rolling and hitting the wall with his right side, the UZI in his right hand, had flung himself behind a giant analog computer installation. Knowing he had to turn himself in order to get a clear shot at the group of men at the end of the room, he glanced up and—surprise! —looked directly into the astonished face of N. G. Merkulov, the GRU agent who, posing as "John Cecil Evers," had helped arrange the kidnap plot.

Completely taken by surprise, Merkulov stood some twenty feet away, behind the computer at its opposite end, his handsome face immobile with confusion. A machine pistol dangled in his hand.

Camellion knew that with the UZI half pinned to the wall, he wouldn't have time to shoot the double agent. He was also too busy with living to die! His left hand flew first to his back, then sailed outward as the fear-stricken Merkulov tried to bring up his weapon. The Russian didn't succeed. The short barrel of the M-pistol was still angled at the floor when the blade of Camellion's commando knife shot into his throat, directly below the chin. Reflex tightened his trigger finger and two slugs spit at the Death Merchant, one sharply grazing the inner thigh of his left leg, the other slicing a deep cut on the outside of his other leg, close to his knee.

Gurgling, his mouth and throat vomiting blood, his eyes

144

rolling crazily, Merkulov grabbed his throat and staggered out into the room, his fingers working along the knife handle like a drunken flute player's. Slipping in his own blood, he fell in front of the Psychotron complex and died.

Yes indeed . . . the vicissitudes of a capricious existence tend to be prodigiously startling in the unexpectedness with which they often present themselves!—and Camellion knew that if GRU agents were rushing toward him from the end of the large room, he wouldn't have time to turn before firing. Reversing the UZI and holding it backward, he pointed the barrel over his left shoulder and opened fire, swinging the barrel.

Screams! The thud of bodies striking the floor! And a strange silence! The generator was no longer running. Either someone had turned it off, or else some of the slugs from the wild firing had silenced it.

Richard turned himself in the narrow space and saw not only four bodies on the floor, between the Booster and the Generator—as well as the corpse he had flung into the room—but more men rushing toward him from the end of the large lab, four of them wearing Red Army insignia on their sleeves, and all of them armed with rifles, except one man, apparently an officer, who carried a machine pistol. Three other men, not wearing insignia, carried high powered M-pistols.

The Death Merchant almost felt pity for the Commie crackpots as he opened fire, his UZI chattering faster than a group of old maids discussing an X-rated movie! He watched his slugs chewing into them and knocking them over like pins in a bowling alley. Just to be doubly certain, he stitched the fallen Russians again with steel, smashing from them what little life remained.

Another surprise! Richard heard the raging voice of Colonel Kagorin screaming above the whirring of the electrical Booster, "VICTOR, HE'S KILLED COLONEL VERTES-BIESK AND THE OTHERS! TRY TO GET TO THE SIDE OF THE BASTARD AND SHOOT HIS LEGS OFF! I WANT THE SON OF A BITCH ALIVE!"

Smiling, Camellion peered around the corner of the computer bank. Alexis Kagorin was apparently behind the Booster, whose giant balance wheel was spinning furiously. And then the Russian espionage chief stuck his head up, his hate-filled eyes two burning coals, his mouth twisted in a hideous snarl.

145

Camellion didn't even bother to aim the UZI. He merely pulled the trigger, moving and aiming the weapon by instinct. Click! The machine gun had exhausted its ammo, the clip empty. Feeling stupid and cursing Fate, the Death Merchant dodged back and rammed in a fresh clip as Colonel Kagorin pointed an odd-looking weapon in his direction.

Richard had moved in the nick of time. There was no sound from Kagorin's weapon, not as much as a whisper. There was only an intense beam of amplified light that was suddenly there, that bridged the space between Kagorin and the Death Merchant in less than a twinkling of an eye. Instantly, a perfectly round hole appeared in the back of the computer, not two inches from the tip of Camellion's nose, the solid-appearing beam of light hitting the wall and popping the concrete with a noise that sounded like a firecracker exploding.

A laser! Kagorin has some kind of laser gun! Richard had not forgotten the man whom Kagorin had called "Victor!" Where was he? Alexis had told "Victor" to get to the side of the Death Merchant, and order that indicated Victor must be somewhere behind the Psychotron device, either behind the long control panel directly across the room, or else behind the bottom section of the "L"-shaped device at the end of the room.

Another short hiss as metal sizzled! Another hole magically appeared in the back of the Psychotron, the molten metal dribbling from the edges, only a few inches above Camellion, who was crawling toward the end of the computer, which by now was making weird sputtering noises from the laser's having eaten into its complicated circuits.

ZIPPPPPPPP!—and still another hole appeared. Once more the concrete popped!

Coming to the end of the computer, Camellion saw that the bottom section of the Psychotron—the short leg of the "L"—was almost half as wide as it was long, about seven feet. He also saw that there was an open space between the end of the computer and the end of the Psychotron—another six or seven feet.

Hmmmmm! Toss a grenade at Kagorin? No, I might kill him, and I want to do that with my bare hands.

Richard slipped a few cartridges from a loose machine gun clip and tossed them toward the opposite end of the computer. ZIPPPPPPP! Kagorin fired again, a bright beam of light

146

slicing through the computer a few feet above where the cartridges had hit the floor. Camellion jumped the short distance from computer to Psychotron, and then noticed that a metal ladder, fastened to the end of the last bank, led up to the top of the device, which he judged to be about twelve feet high. He hesitated, trying to decide what course of action to take—and where was Victor?

Again, Camellion heard Alexis Kagorin call out. "VICTOR! THE BASTARD'S AT THE END OF THE COMPUTER! WATCH OUT FOR HIM!"

Wisely not revealing his position, Victor did not answer. Standing at the end of the Psychotron, the Death Merchant knew the man had to be behind either the short or long section of the Psychotron! But which one?

Groaning slightly, Camellion popped two phenoral tablets into his mouth. The pain in his legs from Merkulov's near hits was agonizing, although the cuts made by the slugs weren't serious. Nonetheless, the thigh graze was a deep one and had bled profusely, to the extent that blood had seeped down his leg into his left boot.

Trapped! Feeling that he was cornered, Richard decided to investigate the top of the Psychotron. He began climbing the ladder. No sooner was he half-way up than Kagorin let fly with a laser shot, this time the beam drilling through a section of the Psychotron and searing Camellion's right side, almost causing him to scream and fall from the ladder; but he managed to climb the rest of the way up and stick his head over the top. Not bad at all! The top of the Psychotron was also L-shaped, the ladder leading to the bottom of the "L," which was perhaps four feet wide, the front two feet wide and rising another three feet. Hurriedly, his rubber soles silent against the metal rungs of the ladder, Camellion climbed on top of the Psychotron, keeping low and shielding himself behind the front wall section of the device.

The Psychotron had been turned off after the Israeli bombing had destroyed its wave-antenna. Even so, it still spat and sputtered internally as Colonel Kagorin, in his blind hatred for Richard Camellion, began filling the end full of laser holes!

Where is Victor? Slowly, Richard crawled along the top of the Psychotron, inching his way along. Except for the whirring of the Booster and its rapidly spinning balance wheel, there was no noise. It was obvious to Richard what

Victor was doing: playing it cool . . . waiting and listening.

Alexis Kagorin, not knowing the exact location of Victor Gulyaiev, his second in command, had stopped firing. Of course, he more than realized he could riddle the Psychotron with laser shots, in the hope that a random beam would find Camellion. And the hell with Victor! A *kolkhozniki* he certainly was, but still a good agent who followed orders—and a faithful Party member!

Kagorin would have liked to riddle the board in dozens of places, but his own code of honor would not permit him to risk Victor's life; yet, in spite of his insane hatred of the Death Merchant, a wave of apprehension washed through Kagorin's consciousness . . . an oscillation of fear, but not from cowardice, not from the thought of dying. It was the realization that he might lose his chance to kill the Death Merchant that made dread loom large in Alexis!

After the bombing and after the Psychotron antenna had come tumbling down, a great emptiness had filled Kagorin, combined with the sickening awareness that he might as well be dead. A realist, knowing his career was over, he welcomed death, but only if he could take the Death Merchant with him; and this feeling that all that made life worth living was gone made him strangely invulnerable. He was absolutely certain he had no future, but at the same time, there was stark reality in the grim present. And so Alexis Kagorin waited, a man with a scar festering on his brain, a man who must have loved somebody once . . . waited and listened for the slightest sound from the Psychotron, his finger on the trigger of the laser gun.

Richard Camellion came to the end of the top of the Psychotron and, very cautiously, peered downward over the edge, staring at the narrow space between the wall and the long section of the device. The space between wall and Psychotron was empty. So—Victor had to be behind the short section. Richard also noticed that another ladder was attached to this end of the Psychotron, not that he'd be able to use it to climb down and get to the back of Victor. To even try such a move would expose him to Colonel Kagorin, provided the GRU chief was still behind the Booster.

Camellion crawled back several feet and, somehow, managed to turn himself around. Knowing the UZI was useless in such close quarters, he pulled out a .357 and peered over the edge. There was Victor, a Zortov automatic pistol in his hand ... twelve feet below and five feet in front of him.

Poor fellow! thought Camellion. From the breast pocket of his jungle fatigues, he pulled a four-foot length of coiled parachute cord. It was a shame he couldn't use a knife on Victor, but he couldn't. His knife was sticking in the throat of N. G. Merkulov—and if he shot the man, the sound would reveal his position to Colonel Kagorin, who would then proceed to laser him to pieces before he had time to change position.

I'll strangle the joker! Once more Camellion looked over the edge. Super cautious, Victor Gulyaiev had moved ahead only a few feet. With the ends of the cord wrapped around each hand, the Death Merchant sprang from the top, the garrote ready for the taste of warm flesh.

Victor turned in that instant the cord fell over his head and the Death Merchant began tightening it around his throat. The urge for life, the wild desire to live, made Victor drop the Zortov as his hands flew to his throat, in an effort to pull away the cord now digging into his windpipe and cutting off his air. He might as well have tried to move the Rock of Gibralter with his fingernails! Making hideous gurging noises, he struggled as if possessed by a dozen devils, his eyes bugged to the extent it seemed miraculous they didn't pop right out of his head ... his tongue extended full length, to its very roots.

He was about to use the old Karate technique of slamming an elbow into Camellion's stomach and at the same time stomping on his instep. He should have known better!

Wisely, the Death Merchant moved his head down through his arms, and then, turning slightly so that his hands went behind his head, bent over, a quick motion that jerked Victor off his feet and placed his back against Camellion's, his entire weight supported by the tightening garrote. He shuddered and died, becoming limp within seconds.

Camellion let the body sag to the floor, then moved to the end of the Psychotron, only five feet away. Hoping his plan would work, he yelled out, "I've just strangled your boy, Kagorin. Your turn's next!"

Camellion then turn and ran to the opposite end of the Psychotron, just as Kagorin began drilling the end from which Camellion had called.

ZIPPPP! ZAPPPPPP! ZZZZZZZIPPPPPPP!

149

The Death Merchant jerked his head toward the welcome sound—gunfire coming from behind the closed door at the far end of the lab—from that section where "The Box" had revealed numerous small rooms. Ha! Jock and the commandos had found another entrance and were attacking!

Richard poked his head around the corner and stared down the narrow space between the wall and the long section of Psychotron banks. At the end of the narrow passage he could see part of the Booster—and still Colonel Kagorin continued to fire at the other end, indicating that he didn't suspect what Camellion had in mind.

With incredible speed, his Magnum poised for firing, the Death Merchant ran down the passageway and looked around the corner of the last control panel.

Alexis Kagorin had moved out from behind the Booster and was walking slowly toward the Psychotron, pausing every few seconds to drill it with a laser beam, so intent on killing the Death Merchant that he apparently hadn't heard the gunfire coming from the technicians' living quarters—or else was ignoring it!

Alexis moved a few more steps, his face a twisted mask of diabolical fury. The Death Merchant holstered his .357 and waited. Kagorin took a few more steps toward the Psychotron. *Zippppppp*—and turned his back slightly.

The Death Merchant jumped the GRU colonel, leaping out from behind the corner of the Psychotron and throwing an arm around Kagorin's beefy neck. With the flat edge of his other hand, he chopped Kagorin's wrist, forcing open the man's hand. The laser fell to the floor and Camellion kicked it across the room.

Kagorin didn't lose wind by snarling obscenities. With a burst of brute strength he flung the Death Merchant forward, over his shoulder. Richard hit the floor on his back, his senses reeling, the wind knocked from his lungs. He rolled over just in time to avoid Kagorin, who was attempting to stomp on his belly with both feet. Then Kagorin kicked at Richard's head, aiming for the temple. Dodging, the Death Merchant did a quick double roll and scrambled to his feet, quickly throwing a right handed chop blow at Kagorin's throat—missed, but connected with a left pointed-hand jab, one that speared the espionage boss directly below the Adam's apple. But the blow didn't even slow him down! Charging in like a runaway express train, Kagorin screamed, "I'm go-

150

ing to break your back in a dozen places!" Saliva dribbled from the corners of his mouth, and his eyes . . . staring and blazing . . . clearly indicated the madman he had become. And he moved with incredible speed.

Grabbing Camellion around the waist, he lifted him off his feet and began squeezing, turning around as he did so. Richard immediately counter-attacked by slapping Kagorin over the ears—as hard as he could—with the heels of his palms, setting up a pressure that even a homicidal maniac couldn't tolerate. He released the Death Merchant, his hands flying to his ears, and then once more he tried to grab him in a bear hold.

But now it was Halloween time for the Death Merchant—all tricks and no treats. Grabbing Kagorin by his shirt front, the Death Mercant fell backwards, deliberately pulling the Russian GRU chief with him. As they fell, Camellion doubled up both legs and pushed out against Kagorin's middle with all his strength, sending the espionage boss flying over his head as he fell on his back.

Constantine Alexis Kagorin—seeing for only a second his final destination—squealed like a pig stuck with a slaughtering knife, a high pitched scream of disbelief that was abruptly cut off by a loud thud as his body flew directly into the furiously spinning balance wheel of the Booster and was immediately thrown off, rejected as an intruder and sent tumbling sideways into space. Cut and mangled beyond recognition, Kagorin's decapitated corpse—also minus an arm and leg—crashed against the short section of the Psychotron. Then, heavily, it dropped to the floor.

Kagorin's head—a comet with a spraying red tail—had sailed from the balance wheel, hit the computer, bounced off and, like a bowling ball, rolled awkwardly across the floor, stopping only when it collided with the foot of Colonel Vertesbiesk, who was as dead as Kagorin now was. Having spun off from the wheel, Kagorin's arm had landed on the back of another dead GRU agent, while his leg had flown out the doorway blasted earlier by Camellion.

The Death Merchant felt a set of fingers tighten around his wrist, helping him to his feet. Glancing up, he stared into the battle-weary face of Jock Heydecker, next to whom stood Israela. Jock had a bloody handkerchief wrapped around the fleshy part of his right arm and one of Israela's arms was in a make-shift sling. She smiled weakly. "Only a flesh wound," she explained. "But I think the bone's broken."

Jock looked around the giant Psychotron lab which Camellion had turned into a morgue, his gaze fastening on the Psychotron banks. "So that's it!" he exclaimed, smiling. "Well, we'll blow the bloody bastard into a billion pieces."

Israela had removed her helmet, and her long dark hair flowed to her shoulders.

"All the Ivans back there are dead," she said, jerking her head toward the door through which they had just come. "And that includes the technicians. But don't worry. We found Dr. Popvikin and his partner in invention—would you believe it? —hiding under their beds. Bloom and George are guarding them."

"Jock, how many did you lose?" Camellion asked, swallowing two more phenoral tablets. His legs throbbed with pain, and his side—laser-grazed—was blue-white agony.

"Three," Jock replied in a sad voice. "Captain Dafna got it attacking the Russians up top, just before we found the entrance in one of the burned out barracks. Shot through the lungs. He wasn't dead when we left him though."

"Two others were killed when we attacked down here," Israela finished, her face twisting from the pain in her arm.

Jock put his hand on Camellion's shoulder, and his voice shook with tension. "Just before we came in here, one of the men on the surface called me on the walkie talkie. He reported spotting lights in the distance—help from Suez."

"We haven't any time to waste," Israela said simply.

The Death Merchant nodded. "Start slapping RDX packs on the Psychotron. Set the timers for half an hour. I'm going up on the Psychotron and get my shoulder bag. I don't want to leave 'The Box' behind."

Quickly he moved to the ladder at one end, stopping on his way to scoop up the laser weapon. U. S. Army engineers at Aberdeen would want to have a look at such a weapon.

Within fifteen minutes a dozen packs of RDX had been attached to the Psychotron installation, and the little group of commandos was on the surface, preparing to dash through the desert to the waiting helicopters. One of the commandos, who had remained on the surface, had wired the base's ammo dump with explosives, setting the timers for twenty minutes. Five of those minutes were already gone.

To their surprise, they found Captain Dafna standing in

the turret of the T-54 Camellion had captured, leaning against the handrail of the hatch. He had turned the turret, and now the barrel of the 100MM was pointed in the direction from which, far off in the distance, a string of lights was moving.

"We'll help you down, Hayim," Jock said, motioning to Sgt. Bloom to climb up with him on the tank. "Don't worry; we'll get you back home safely."

Captain Dafna smiled weakly and shook his head. "Don't be a fool, Jock," he said, then grimaced from the pain of speaking. "I'm dying—and there's no sense in your lugging back a corpse. I'd only slow you down! I intend to stay here and give the Egyptian column from Suez a welcome with the tank gun. Now get out of here . . . all of you."

Without waiting for a reply, Dafna dropped down into the turret and slammed the hatch, locking it.

Led by the Death Merchant, the small group of commandos started out across the desert. Twenty-three of them had started out—twenty-seven, including the four pilots, but they hadn't taken part in the battle. Now . . . only seven were alive, and all of them wounded.

Dr. Popvikin might have been taking a hike. "I shall want the best of equipment in my laboratory," he said in a haughty voice as they pushed him along over the sand, speaking in the manner of a Roman senator. Every time he opened his mouth, Camellion half expected him to orate in Latin and exhort mythical legions to storm the gates of Carthage. "After all," he finished, "a rich nation like the United States can afford to give me the best . . ."

Sgt. Bloom poked him in the back with the muzzle of an UZI. "If you don't shut up, all you'll get is six feet of sand —MOVE!"

Dr. Popvikin smiled secretly to himself, knowing they wouldn't dare shoot him . . . not unless he attempted to escape. He was too valuable. A realist, he accepted the fact that he was in the hands of the Israelis and, having been told that he was to be flown secretly to the USA, his only concern was that he might not be allowed to continue his scientific experiments.

Doctor Sergeyev also accepted the fact that he was a prisoner, but he remained quiet, moving like a robot, doing as he was told.

Moving as fast as they could, at times almost running, they all knew they had to reach the waiting copters before

153

the relief tanks from Suez reached the area and began shelling them.

Sgt. Bloom was leading them to where he had left Noah Weinstein, the commando who had been shot in the stomach, when they heard the thunderous explosion. The ammo dump had blown up, filling the sky with a bright flash, as well as tracer tracks. They wondered if the explosion might have wrecked the T-54 in which Captain Dafna was waiting, but no one asked the question, none of them wanting to think of Hayim sitting back there, alone . . . waiting for the Egyptians . . . waiting for death.

They came to Weinstein. He was dead, lying face down in the cold sand.

The little group continued to race across the desert, passing burned out T-54s and dead Russians. Even the wind seemed to whisper of death and destruction—more so than usual! For in this emptiness, there was never any hope . . . in this sea of sand where everything was always blowing away by degrees . . . this world where the wind was constantly changing the landscape and not even a dog could help one contain the bitter loneliness of the days.

Panting from exhaustion, Camellion finally said, "We're almost there. Our copter should be over the next rise."

Another shuddering explosion . . . a deep rumble, as though the earth itself were thundering and collapsing in on itself.

"That's the end of the Psychotron lab," Israela said, and even in the darkness Richard could see that she was smiling.

Then—the distant roar of a T-54's 100MM cannon. No one said anything, but they knew that the column from Suez was within range and that Captain Dafna was spreading out the welcome mat.

The seven Israeli commandos and the two Russian scientists climbed to the top of the rise and there, at the bottom of the long slope, was the Frelon troop-carrying helicopter. They boarded without delay, and one of the pilots radioed the other two copters, both the decoy and the stand-by crafts. Again, the same strategy was employed, only this time there was one difference: Now, in order to insure the safe arrival of Dr. Popvikin into Israel, two copters served as decoys.

The Frelon with the small group of commandos and the two Russian scientists lifted off the sands and headed for Ayun

Mussa, the small village on the Sinai side of the Gulf of Suez, its big rotors spinning.

This time the Egyptians were not caught off guard, firing at the copter with anti-aircraft guns and even small arms! Manning the 50-caliber machine guns mounted to the side openings of the fusilage, the Death Merchant and Jock returned the fire, although, as high as they were, they had no way of knowing what they might be hitting.

They were whizzing over the canal and Jock was yelling, "We've made it, laddies! We're almost home!" when a slug, or piece of shrapnel, drilled in through the bottom of the copter and found Richard Camellion.

He felt a terrible stabbing pain in his left side, a hideous flash of agony that knocked him from the machine gun. Then he felt nothing . . . merely a soft kind of velvet darkness . . . black powder puffs that quickly patted his brain into blissful unconsciousness . . . .

EPILOGUE

The late October sun smiled warmly on the settlement that was Nof Ginossar Kibbutz—a blessing to the crops in the fields and to the trees, the latter looking as if they had been there forever. Among the numerous buildings of the settlement, one sat off by itself, a white two-storied building close to an orange grove—the hospital where Camellion and the others had been taken, just in case the GRU, the world-wide Russian espionage apparatus, should decide to send SMERSH assassins after them in reprisal for the destruction of the Psychotron base and the kidnapping of two major Russian scientists.

Standing by the window of the ground floor Reception Room, Israela stood watching a figure move slowly down the walk that led from the hospital.

"Did he tell you where he was going?" she quietly asked.

"No, I thought he might have said something to you," Isser Lev Langbein replied. Standing next to the girl, he too was gazing after Richard Camellion.

"He merely shook my hand and said 'goodbye,'" Israela said. "He said there wasn't any reason for him to remain here, since his wounds had healed. Doctor Kravowitz wanted him to remain at least another week, but"—and she sighed—"you know how determined Richard can be."

"Yes, he has a mind of his own," Langbein said slowly.

Israela's voice was low. "Since the Psychotron base is destroyed, and now that Popvikin and Sergeyev are safely in the United States, I guess he feels there's no point in staying here."

Langbein glanced curiously at the girl, a thin trace of a smile on his lips, a glimmer of sympathy in his kindly eyes.

"Is there?" he asked. "Is there a reason why Camellion should stay in Israel?"

Israela sighed. "No. I don't suppose there is . . ."

Langbein folded his hands behind his back. "It's a stupid world," he said softly, "a violent world filled with greed and hate and prejudice, but now and then there's a tiny flash of justice. I guess you could say that men like the Death Merchant are a part of that justice."

The kibbutz supper bell rang.

Israela did not reply. She continued to watch the receding figure of Richard Camellion. He was turning now, moving through the orange grove, the shadows from the late afternoon sun playing on his back. Presently he was gone.

Israela smiled . . . wondering how she could lose something she never had!

She took Isser by the arm.

"Let's go to supper," she said . . . .